# THE LOST CANOE

To Joshua, who has never been afraid of exploring his new world.

"Be strong and of good courage; be not frightened, neither be dismayed; for the Lord your God is with you wherever you go" (Joshua 1:9).

Thank you for bringing such joy into our lives.

# THE LOST CANOE

## JEFFREY ARCHER NESBIT

**VICTOR BOOKS** ®

A DIVISION OF SCRIPTURE PRESS PUBLICATIONS INC.
USA CANADA ENGLAND

THE CAPITAL CREW SERIES
*Crosscourt Winner*
*The Lost Canoe*
*The Reluctant Runaway*
*Struggle with Silence*

Cover illustration by Kathy Kulin-Sandel

**Library of Congress Cataloging-in-Publication Data**
Nesbit, Jeffrey Asher.
   The lost canoe / by Jeffrey Asher Nesbit.
      p.    cm. — (The Capital crew series)
   Summary: Cally's survival skills are tested and questions about
God answered when he and his brother attend a Christian
summer camp and become lost on a canoe trip.
   ISBN 0-89693-130-7
   [1. Church camps—Fiction.  2. Camps—
Fiction.  3. Survivial—Fiction.  4. Lost children—
Fiction.  5. Brothers—Fiction.  6. Christian life—Fiction.]
I. Title.  II. Series.
PZ7.N4378Lo  1991
[Fic]—dc20
                                         90-27627
                                           CIP
                                           AC

**1  2  3  4  5  6  7  8  9  10**  Printing/Year  95  94  93  92  91

VICTOR BOOKS
A division of SP Publications, Inc.
Wheaton, Illinois 60187

**Chris was way up there.** He'd vanished somewhere in the leaves, several limbs above the one I was on in the gigantic oak tree out behind our house. I vaguely wondered why he was risking his neck.

"I'm still gonna catch you," I hollered up at my younger brother. "You can't hide up there forever."

"Wanna bet?" I heard a muffled voice call down. I couldn't quite pinpoint where it was coming from because there were too many leaves between Chris and me. He was *way* up there.

"What'll you do when it gets dark?" I asked him.

"Stay up here all night, if I have to."

I sighed. It was hopeless. Chris would wait up there until the cows came home, just to avoid me. He was stubborn like that, and foolish enough to climb up where I wouldn't follow in order to stay away from me.

I couldn't really blame him, though. I *was* mad as a hornet. Or, at least, I'd been mad until I'd exhausted myself chasing Chris all around our house, the "barn," trying to catch him.

We'd been playing baseball out back, just the two of us. And he'd deliberately drilled a fastball into my back. Never mind that it was only a tennis ball. It hurt like crazy and I set off after Chris almost the instant after it had happened.

"Hey, Cally," my brother called down at me from the treetop.

"What?" I snapped back.

"I didn't mean to. Really."

"Yeah, sure," I said skeptically.

"The ball just slipped out of my hand," he protested.

"Oh, give me a break," I said darkly. "Admit it. You were aiming at me. You meant to nail me, to punish me for the home run I'd just crushed off you . . . "

"I wasn't, Cally. I swear."

I almost believed him. But not enough to let him off the hook just yet. "Okay," I said reasonably. "I believe you. You can come down now."

I could hear his chuckle. "Uh-uh, no way. You'll kill me if I come down right now."

"But I said I believed you."

"Doesn't matter," Chris said. "You're still gonna kill me."

I didn't say anything right away. I moved off of the perch I'd found in the tree, grabbed hold of a limb just above my head and pulled myself up a little further in the tree. I could hear Chris shifting position above me, anticipating where I was going.

As I stood there in the tree, I couldn't help but think that this was a pretty strange way to spend the first day of summer, the first day of liberation from school.

"Chris, I don't think I can reach you up there," I called out to him.

"So leave. Then I'll come down."

"But I'm not ready to leave just yet," I said moving up to a higher limb.

Chris tried to move away again, but he was beginning to run out of room. "If you come any closer, I'll jump," he said.

I glanced down. It was an awfully long way to the

ground. He'd probably break his leg if he tried it. "No, you won't. It's too far."

"I don't care," he said, a slight quiver in his voice. "It's better than getting murdered by you."

"Chris, Chris," I said soothingly. "I don't see what you're so worried about." I moved up to another limb. The tree started to sway. The leaves began to shake in the general vicinity of where I knew Chris was.

"Don't come any closer!" he warned. "I'll jump."

"You really don't want to do that." I could see pieces of Chris through the leaves now. I was within grabbing distance.

Chris suddenly changed tactics. "If you come any closer, I'll kick you out of the tree. I swear it."

"Now, you wouldn't do that," I answered, looking for a good, solid limb to hang onto just in case he did try to kick me out of the tree. "That wouldn't be nice."

"I will."

Tightly holding onto a sturdy limb, I inched up closer and reached a hand in Chris' direction. With a loud shriek, Chris sent a swift kick through the leaves. He missed, but I could see he was serious about this.

"You're not coming down from there, are you?"

"Nope. Not until you do."

A thought came to me, then. *I may not be able to get him down, but I sure can make him miserable up here,* I reasoned. "Okay, Chris, you win," I said. "I'm getting down."

"And you'll go back in the house?"

"I didn't say that."

"Then I'm stayin' up here."

"Suit yourself."

I climbed down quickly. Once on the ground, I hurried back to the shed behind our house and grabbed two tennis balls and the garden hose.

I made sure the spray nozzle was on tight, connected the hose to the faucet at the back of the house, turned the water on full blast, and hurried back to the oak tree with my ammunition in hand.

Chris hadn't budged. I could actually see him better from the ground because he was up where the leaves were thinner at the top of the tree.

I gave him one last chance. "Chris, if you come down right now, I promise I won't lay a hand on you," I called out.

"No way. I don't believe you."

"All right, then. It's your funeral." I laid the hose on the ground and took aim. I sent the first tennis ball whizzing in Chris' direction. It missed. But the second one connected.

"Hey, cut it out!" he called out. "That hurt."

I didn't say anything. I gathered up the balls and took aim again. This time, they both connected solidly. I tried a third time, and was one for two. "You ready to come down yet?" I asked.

"NO!" Chris shouted, somewhat grimly. I could see that he was reevaluating his position, though.

I picked up the hose. I squeezed the handle on the nozzle. A jet of water issued forth. I let the water cascade high over the tree and shower down onto Chris. Then I aimed it directly at him, soaking him.

"I can stay here all day, Chris," I called out.

"So can I," he answered, his voice again quivering slightly.

I let the water shoot up at him for a little while longer, and finally decided to call it quits. Enough was enough. When Chris had his mind made up, that was that. There was no way he'd budge. I could see that.

But I wasn't about to let him off the hook so easily. "I'm not through with you yet," I warned him.

"What're you doin'?" he yelled as I carried the hose back to the shed.

"You'll see!" I yelled back as I closed the shed and began to walk towards the back door of the house.

"What is it?"

"Just wait," I answered, and then bolted through the door. Chuckling to myself, I made my way to the living room, where Jana and Karen were watching some goofy soap opera.

I plopped down in a chair. I wondered how long it would take Chris to figure out that I wasn't coming back after him.

We were into our second soap when I heard the door out back creak open slowly. I smiled to myself. Good, old Chris. He'd waited up there until he was *absolutely* sure I wasn't coming back.

"You're dead now!" I called out. The door slammed. There was a quick, staccato beat of footsteps on the stairs. A second door—the one to our bedroom loft— slammed upstairs. I heard Chris flip the lock on.

"You'll have to come out for dinner," I yelled.

"No, I won't," said a muffled voice. "I've got two candy bars."

I just shook my head in amazement. If there was anyone with more determination than Chris, I sure hadn't met him. I don't think he would ever give up, no matter what the odds or what the circumstances.

A strange thought came to me. If I was ever really in a jam, I'd want Chris there with me. He'd climb any mountain, no matter how steep, if he had to get to the other side. Or toil for hours to remove some obstacle.

That was Chris, stubborn and persistent beyond words. It could drive you crazy. But in a really tight spot, there wasn't anyone else I'd want with me. No one else in the world.

**It was funny,** but I guess I wasn't really surprised. It was just like him, anyway.

My crumb-bum of a father had driven all the way to Indianapolis to see me play Evan Grant for the finals of the National Indoor Tennis Championship, had vowed to return to our family, and then had never shown his face again. Not for months.

Mom hadn't believed me right away when I'd told her that Dad had shown up and confronted me in the shadows behind the tennis courts in Indianapolis. It did seem pretty strange, the more I thought about it.

And I'd been thinking about it a lot lately. Why had he chosen me? Why hadn't he gone to Karen, who always listened to him, who probably still believed at least some of the lies he told? How come he hadn't tried to see Mom, like he'd vowed? Where was he?

I'd waited until we were driving back to Washington before I told Mom that Dad had said he was coming back and he wanted her to forgive him.

Mom had started crying, softly at first and then louder as she got angry. And, boy, did she get angry. We had to pull the car over and sit on the side of the road for a little bit, she was so angry. I thought she was going to pull the steering wheel out of the car.

I guess she'd held it inside so long, all those feelings towards what my father had done.

"He *snuck* on the court, where no one could see him, and said all those things to you?" she'd finally managed when she'd stopped sobbing.

I'd nodded. "Yeah, and he looked awful, Mom. He'd been drinking."

"He was drunk?" she'd said, the anger edging back into her voice.

"I think so," I'd said. "Actually, I'm pretty sure he was. He smelled really awful."

Mom had closed her eyes. I'm sure she was praying, asking God for strength and peace. "If he talks to you again, Cally, tell him to talk to me," she'd said finally. "I don't want him trying to work through you kids."

Karen had spoken up, then. "He called me a couple of times, Mom," she'd said.

She'd looked back and forth between Karen and me, like we'd both lost our minds. "And you didn't tell me?" she'd asked Karen.

"I . . . I didn't know how to," Karen had pleaded. "He said you'd never forgive him for what he'd done . . . "

Mom had just nodded, her face grim with controlled fury. "Well, he's wrong," she'd said. "I'll forgive him. But that doesn't mean I want him back in this family."

But my father hadn't come back, at least not yet, to ask our mother for forgiveness and to try to return to our family. Like a bad dream, he just lingered somewhere on the edges of our minds, never quite there but always just a thought away.

I wasn't totally sure how Mom would react if she saw him. *I think she'd forgive him. I think I would, too.* Now that I'd become a Christian, I was beginning to lose some of my hatred for him. Some, but not all. He was still a lousy skunk, no matter what.

**Aunt Franny came and sat with the kids** the first
Saturday of the summer so Mom could drive Chris and
me to a camp we were going to for two weeks.

It was bright and clear when we left. You could feel
the day just starting to heat up, like it always does at
the beginning of the summer. The grass was still wet
with morning dew.

We drove on the interstate highway that heads
west out of Washington, D.C. In a way, it reminded
me of the drive nine months earlier, after my father
had left us high and dry in Alabama and Mom had
moved the seven kids up to Uncle Teddy and Aunt
Franny's house while she looked for a job.

Boy, that seemed like it was years ago. Mom's new
job at the State Department — where she showed for-
eign dignitaries around the place — was a neat one.
And the family had gotten used to the fact that our
father wasn't likely to come back.

The hills started to get steeper about an hour into
the drive. We got off the interstate and started to
make our way into West Virginia. The towns all
seemed small in comparison to Washington.

I always wondered what people did in these towns.
Where do they work? Where does everybody go to
school?

"They work on farms, or in places they have to drive

to for quite a ways," Mom answered when I asked.

"But what about school?" I asked.

"Oh, there's usually one school somewhere that all the kids in the county go to," she said. "I went to a school like that."

"In Alabama?"

She nodded. "It was really terrible if you were the first one on the school bus. You'd end up driving around for an hour, picking all the other kids up . . . "

"Yeah, but I'll bet it gave you a chance to get your homework done," Chris said.

Mom and I laughed. Leave it to Chris to see the bright side in any rotten situation. "And when it's still dark outside, how're you gonna see your books?" I asked.

Chris shrugged. "You bring your flashlight, of course."

It was hopeless. He'd find an answer to every challenge. I leaned back in the seat and watched the countryside roll by.

The camp was nestled in some hills northwest of Petersburg, West Virginia, which I figured was some real small town like all the others we were passing through. I was wrong, as usual. Petersburg was pretty big. It even had a Pizza Hut.

Mom glanced at the road map as we left Petersburg, then took a side road and began to angle towards a tall mountain to the north.

"Look at that," I said, pointing towards the mountain, which seemed to be quite a bit taller than the others in the area.

"It's Mount Argus," Mom said. "It's one of the tallest mountains in West Virginia."

"Hey! I know that name," Chris exclaimed.

"What name?" I asked.

"Argus," he answered. "We were reading mythology in class, and Argus was this giant with a hundred eyes. He was a guardian, or something like that. He could see in all directions, all at once. It was pretty neat. But then he died."

I snorted. "If he was a guardian, and he had a hundred eyes, then how'd he die?"

"There was this son of Zeus. Hermes, I think. He was like the messenger of the gods. He was real fast, and real smart. But to get close to Argus, he pretended that he wasn't a god and snuck up on him."

"Snuck up on him?"

"Yeah, he pretended he was this country bumpkin. Then, when he was close, he told Argus this story that put him to sleep. Put all 100 of his eyes to sleep, I mean. Then he killed him, and one of the other gods put all 100 eyes into the tail of the peacock."

"That's a pretty goofy story," I told Chris.

"Yeah, I guess so," he agreed. "But it makes you wonder, when you look at a peacock's tail. Doesn't it?"

"No, it doesn't," I laughed.

We drove through the countryside in silence. It was interesting. Once you got off the main roads, the land seemed harsh and forbidding. *It must be hard to make a living off this land,* I thought.

The houses were few and far between here. And where there were houses, you could only just catch glimpses of them from the road. Most were tucked away behind hills.

There were dogs at most of them as well, the kind of dogs that could chase a car and keep up with it for a good half mile or so. I was glad we weren't trying to ride bicycles through here.

Chris spotted the camp first. He caught a glimpse of

the small mountain lake that was part of it. "Through there," he said, pointing excitedly.

"I can see that, Chris," Mom said patiently.

The road ended right at the camp's entrance, which was marked by a gate and a simple wooden archway with a hand-lettered sign that read "Camp Agape." The gate was open. Mom slowed down some as she entered.

"What's *agape?*" Chris asked, pronouncing it like it rhymed with "grape."

"It's a Greek word for 'love,' " Mom answered. "In the early Christian church, it was used to describe what we now call Holy Communion."

"Communion," Chris said thoughtfully. "That's with the bread and wine in church, right?"

"Yes, that's right," Mom said, with only a flicker of a smile. "It celebrates what Jesus said at the Last Supper."

Chris, however, had already lost interest. His eyes were suddenly riveted on a small pasture where a few kids were riding horses. They were obviously just beginners, because they were only walking the horses. Chris couldn't take his eyes off them, though.

"Wow, that's really neat," he said. "Can I do that?"

"I'm sure you will at some point, Chris," Mom said. "I think you'll need to get settled first."

The camp was pretty big. The lake had a long dock that ran out towards the middle. There were a whole bunch of canoes tied to it. Next to the dock, there was a roped-off section that served as a swimming area, complete with two diving boards.

Off to one side, there was a picnic area and a huge campfire with benches that ringed it. As we drove towards a building that the signs said was the camp headquarters, I spotted a volleyball court, an archery range, a basketball court, and a small soccer field.

Log-cabin dormitories stretched off in either direction. As we got out of the car, two very distinct smells hit me. One was the sweet smell of the pine trees all around us. The other was what seemed to be smoked ham, coming from the building directly in front of us.

"Man, am I hungry," I said to Chris as we got out of the car and limbered up. My legs were stiff from the long drive.

"Yeah, me too," he answered. "I wonder when lunch is."

Mom didn't take long to sign us in. She walked with us as we carried our bags over to our room in the dormitory. She hadn't really said a whole lot during the drive, so I couldn't tell what she was thinking.

Chris had his eyes peeled the whole time we were walking. He just kept glancing from one knot of kids doing something to the next. I thought he was going to just drop his bags at any instant and head over to one of the groups.

When we'd gotten to our room, Mom sat down beside me on the bed as I was unpacking. She leaned over and whispered in a low voice, so only I could hear, "Cally, you watch out for him. I mean it."

"I will. Don't worry," I whispered back.

"I know you will," she said, giving my arm a reassuring squeeze. "But you know how impetuous Chris can be. He's liable to do just about anything that pops into his mind."

"I'll stay close by," I said, glancing over at Chris, who was just pulling wrinkled clothes from a duffel bag and throwing them in drawers at random.

"Good," she said firmly. Mom stood up and added, in a louder voice, "I'm leaving, Chris. You two have a good time."

Chris broke off from his unpacking, hurried over, and gave Mom a quick hug. "See ya," he said to her. "Don't forget to come back and pick us up in two weeks."

"I'll remember," she said, mussing up Chris' hair playfully. Chris ducked away.

Mom turned to me. "I mean it. You watch over him," she said in one ear as we embraced briefly. "Promise you'll pay close attention?"

"I promise," I answered solemnly, wondering just how tough it would actually be to keep track of him.

"All right, then, I'm off," she said. Mom lingered at the doorway for a brief moment, and then left.

A sudden, crushing weight of responsibility seemed to settle on my shoulders. I tried to shrug off the feeling, but it wouldn't leave.

I glanced over at Chris, who had almost finished unpacking and was ready to bolt out the door for one of the ongoing activities. I hadn't even opened my bags yet. It could be a long two weeks.

**They divided the camp that afternoon.** Half of us became the Elks team, the other half the Bears.

Then the counselors pulled out just about the biggest rope I've ever seen, laid it across an imaginary "no-man's" land in the center of the camp, and started the biggest tug-of-war I've ever seen.

I was on the Elks, Chris was on the Bears team. I could see him toiling mightily toward the end of the rope on his side. I was sandwiched in between two girls who began screaming about two minutes into the contest and didn't let up until it was over.

It was funny to watch, actually. Just when one team would start to get an advantage and the flag in the center of the rope would start to inch towards one side, the other would put on a fierce display of power and pull it back towards the center again.

This went on for quite a while. By the end, we were all so weary that we could hardly pull. But I could still see Chris straining for all he was worth, urging those around him not to give up, to keep on pulling.

The Bears finally won, largely because they had a few others just like Chris who wouldn't quit. Once our first team member was pulled into the "no-man's" land and had to let go of the rope, it went quickly. Within seconds, they'd pulled the rope and most of our team across the line.

I just lay on my back for a few moments afterward. Suddenly a body came hurtling through the air and landed with a "thump" on top of me. I just barely had time to put my hands up to protect myself.

"What a major wimp," Chris said as he gave me an elbow to my rib cage.

"You're right, I am," I said, deciding not to protest. "You guys just gave up."

"No, we didn't. You just pulled harder."

"That means I'm stronger than you."

"Oh, yeah?"

Chris started to ease away. I grabbed his arm. "Yeah, it does," he said, and then tried to bolt away. I held fast.

"Well, we'll have to see about that." I pinned his arm back and grabbed him around the waist. He put up a fierce struggle, but I succeeded in pinning him to the ground underneath me.

"Hey, get off!" Chris half-yelled, his voice muffled beneath me. "You're crushing me, you fatso."

"Fatso?"

"Yeah, you're killing me. Get off."

"Fatso?"

"You heard me," Chris said bravely.

I pressed a little harder. Not too much, but just enough to make him think. "You sure I'm a fatso?" I asked.

Chris went limp, like a rag doll. I knew this was one of his favorite tactics, when he was on the defensive like this. I had to be wary. I had to anticipate a sneak-attack.

"All right, I give," he said with a heavy sigh.

"Good," I answered, relaxing a little. That proved to be a costly mistake.

"But you're still a fatso!" Chris said, suddenly heaving with his legs, throwing me off to one side. I couldn't react quickly enough, and he wriggled free.

Before I could pick my weary body off the ground, Chris had bolted in the direction of one of the camp counselors. I hustled over to him, but he was already standing just to one side of the counselor. I knew there was nothing I could do. He'd outfoxed me. This time.

"So, what's next?" I heard Chris ask.

The counselor was an older boy in his late teens, I guessed. He had a thick, black mat of curls on his head that seemed to grow in all directions at once. It reminded me a little of Medusa, that woman in myths who had all those snakes growing on her head.

"Oh, I don't know," this kid answered. "Got any suggestions?"

Chris glanced over at me. "Yeah, let's go somewhere else. Anyplace but here."

"Why's that?" he asked.

"Oh, just because," Chris answered.

The kid followed Chris' nervous gaze in my direction. He smiled, knowingly. "That your older brother?" he asked Chris, who just nodded, keeping his eyes locked on my approach.

I didn't really have anything in mind. I figured I'd just let Chris sweat a little. Chris started to edge behind the counselor as I came near the two of them.

"Don't come any closer, Cally," Chris warned.

"Or what?" I sneered.

"Or my friend here will pulverize you," Chris said.

"Pulverize me?"

This kid, who had a crooked nose and equally crooked teeth to match, broke into a huge grin. "Yeah, I might," he said, taking Chris' side. "You never know."

I cocked my head to one side, appraising Chris' new friend. "You wouldn't," I said. "You'd get kicked out of camp."

"I guess you're right," he said, laughing. I liked his laugh. It was a deep, guttural, belly laugh, the kind that makes you want to join in. "I wouldn't want to get kicked out on my first day here." He stretched out a hand in my direction. I took it uncertainly. "My name's Jonathon Astor. Most people call me Jon."

"Cally James," I mumbled as I shook his hand.

"Pleased to meet you," he said, then turned to Chris. "And you are?"

"Chris James," he answered.

"Where y'all from?" Jon asked us.

"Washington, D.C.," I answered. "How 'bout you?"

"I just finished my freshman year at UVA."

"UVA?" Chris asked.

"Sorry," Jon said, "the University of Virginia, in Charlottesville. It's right down the road. My folks live in Roanoke."

Chris and I nodded meekly. College seemed so remote, so far away. I could hardly even force myself to think about the eighth grade next year.

"So what's next?" Chris blurted out.

Jon gave me a funny look. "Is he always this impatient?"

"Yep, about everything."

"It must drive you crazy."

"Just a little," I said, edging still closer to Chris while he wasn't paying attention. "But when he gets out of line, I just . . . "

Chris saw my move coming, but he was a fraction of a second too late. I caught his backside with a hard "flick" of my fingers as he tried to get out of the way.

"Ouch!" he yelled. "That hurt."

"I'm glad."

"You'll pay for that," he said darkly.

Jon just stood there, not quite sure what to do. "Why don't you get back?" he asked Chris.

"You crazy?" Chris answered with a cockeyed glance. "He'd kill me. I'll do somethin' about it later."

"In your dreams," I said wryly.

I glanced at Jon. He was looking off in the distance, towards the lake. "I've got an idea," he said. "You guys interested in taking a canoe out on the lake? We could take it down one of the tributaries . . . "

"Yeah, let's do it!" Chris said exuberantly.

"You up for it?" Jon asked me. I nodded. "All right, then. We have about two hours of free time to kill until dinner. Let's roll."

Chris and I picked out the canoe while Jon went over to the camp's main building and signed us out. As usual, we disagreed on the choice. I chose a big, sturdy-looking canoe. Chris chose a sleek but slightly unsteady one.

"We're takin' mine," Chris insisted.

"No way. We'll drown in yours. You'll get all carried away and tip us over."

"Nah. We'll zip through the water in mine."

"Until we hit a rock, or until you catch your oar on a tree branch and flip us over."

Chris cast a disparaging look at my choice. "We'll never get yours away from the dock."

"Sure we will. And mine won't flip over like yours."

"Yeah, because it'll never move. We'll just sit here and admire the view."

"Momentum," I offered. "Once we get rolling . . . "

"What about comin' back upstream?" Chris interrupted.

"Well, the same principle."

"We're goin' in mine," Chris said firmly. "I'm not gonna be stuck down at the end of some creek because your tank of a canoe couldn't make it back."

I sighed. He'd won this round. But I wasn't about to give in. "We'll let Jon choose."

Jon didn't hesitate. "Why would you want to take that monster out?" he asked, pointing at the canoe I'd chosen. "That's for kids who just sort of float around the lake. It's guaranteed not to sink, under any circumstance."

Chris started giggling. "I tried to tell him, but he wouldn't listen. As usual."

I kept silent. I'd clearly goofed, but perhaps there was a way out of it yet. "Isn't it better to be safe?" I tried.

Jon shrugged. "Sure, but you don't have to go overboard. No pun intended. . . . "

"Huh?" asked Chris.

"Overboard," I said.

"Oh, I get it," Chris said, nodding.

Jon grabbed the end of the canoe Chris had chosen and eased it into the water. He threw two oars and three lifejackets he'd brought with him into the canoe. "Climb in. I'll push us out," he directed. Chris and I both complied.

The canoe glided through the still lake. Little ripples gurgled out on both sides. I saw a fish dart off to one side. The sudden movement of the boat startled a few ducks swimming nearby. One of them bolted for the air with a loud "quack, quack, quack" and the others quickly followed.

There are moments when everything seems just as it should be, as if you are doing exactly as God intended you to do, that there is absolutely nothing else you should, or could, be doing at the moment.

This was one of those moments. I glanced at Chris, who was just staring at the water dumbly as it slipped beneath the canoe. I wondered fleetingly if he ever had thoughts like that.

"So is anybody planning to paddle here, or are we just going to drift around for a while," Jon asked, breaking the reverie.

Chris jerked to attention, grabbed a paddle, and dipped it gingerly into the water. I just stared at the other paddle. Jon had only brought two oars.

Jon started smiling at me. "You don't seriously think I'm going to paddle, do you?" he asked me. It was then that I noticed the choice of seats in the canoe. Jon had strategically placed himself in the center. Chris was at the front, and I pulled up the rear.

"Great," I said aloud. "Not only do I have to paddle, I have to steer, too."

"Yeah, and you better not mess up," offered Chris.

I scooped up a handful of water and flicked it in Chris' direction. *"You'd* better pull your weight," I said.

"Don't worry about me," he answered, shaking drops of water out of his hair. "Just keep us off the rocks."

Sighing, I picked up the oar and put it in the water on the side opposite Chris' oar. "Try to keep up with me, Chris," I said.

"No problem," he answered, though he cast a wary glance back at me to make sure I wasn't planning to set an Olympic record for canoeing.

It took us a while, but Chris and I finally developed a rhythm. That's the only way you can make a canoe move through the water with any speed. Both paddlers have to work together, pulling at the same time and dipping their paddles at the same time.

I discovered that it was easier to steer by rowing extra hard to nudge us in one direction or the other, rather than stop paddling and hold my oar in the water like a rudder.

We made it across the lake in no time at all. As we began to approach the shore on the other side, Jon pointed off to the right. "Let's try over there," he said. "One of the other counselors said there's a creek that goes back a ways."

Chris saw it first—he always seems to see things just slightly sooner than anyone else around—and directed us towards it. As we began to drift towards it, I noticed that it seemed to be heading off towards Mount Argus.

"Hey, Jon," I asked, "this lake, where does it come from?"

Jon jerked his head towards Mount Argus. "I'm sure it's maintained by the runoff from the mountain," he said. We're on one of the tributaries that comes out of the mountain. There are probably dozens of them that feed into the lake, many of them underground."

"So we're going uphill right now?" asked Chris.

"Sort of," Jon said, laughing.

"I thought it seemed hard," Chris said.

"Don't worry, it'll be downhill when we turn around," said Jon.

"Doesn't help right now," Chris huffed in the middle of a stroke.

I looked back at the mountain. It didn't seem quite as high from where we were now. I guess it's all in your perspective. A thought occurred to me.

"So if you were standing at the top of the mountain, and you were lost, you could find your way back by following one of the streams down the mountain until it fed into the lake?" I asked.

"Sure," nodded Jon. "That's the way the Indians made 'roads.' They followed the streams. The settlers made their way out west by following the rivers."

"That's cool," Chris said.

"Actually," Jon continued, "that's a principle you can always follow in the woods. Eventually, every river leads to *somewhere*. If you follow it, you don't need a compass because you know it's going somewhere. You don't have to worry about wandering in circles."

"So if I ditch the two of you, I can just follow the river back to the camp?" Chris joked.

"You'd never ditch me," I said menacingly.

"Wanna bet?" Chris said.

"Anytime," I said.

There was a sudden movement off to the side of the boat. Some kind of an animal bolted from the creek and crashed headlong into the brush that grew along the side of the river.

"What was *that?*" asked Chris.

"Probably a muskrat," Jon said. "There are a lot of them along here."

"Maybe it was a mountain lion," Chris said.

Jon shook his head. "Nah, not at this time of day. And there's probably only one mountain lion roaming this entire mountain range. Doubtful that you'd see him fighting his way through the brush to drink at a dinky creek like this."

"What do you mean?" I asked, curious.

"Well, mountain lions stake out their territory, just like all predators," Jon said. "and in this part of the country, that territory is really wide."

"So where would we see one?" asked Chris.

"Oh, you might see one anywhere," Jon said. "Although there aren't very many left on the East Coast. There are more of them out West."

"Have you heard of one around here?" I asked.

"You know, it's funny, but one of the counselors was talking about that this morning when I came in," Jon said thoughtfully. "He'd been into Petersburg to shop and one of the locals said they'd heard of a mountain lion that had moved into the region. Apparently one of the farmers had spotted it on a mountain crag."

"Yikes," Chris said. "What do we do if we see one?"

"Hide," I said, laughing nervously.

"Actually, mountain lions — and bears, too, I guess — don't hunt humans," Jon said. "I'm not sure why. I guess something instinctively tells them we can prey on them just as easily as they can on us, so they try to steer clear and go after the deer and ground game."

"You sure seem to know a lot about this stuff," Chris said over his shoulder.

"I'm supposed to, remember? That's why they pay me the big bucks," Jon said with a chuckle. "But it's really because my folks are into this kind of thing. They come out to West Virginia all the time, just to hike around."

An image of my father, the crumb-bum, wandering through the hills of West Virginia passed through my mind for an instant. It really struck me as funny. Wicked funny. For what must have seemed like no apparent reason to Chris and Jon, I just burst out laughing.

"What's so *funny?*" Chris asked.

Both of them were staring at me like I'd lost my mind. "Oh, nothing," I said, trying to keep from laughing anymore. "I was just trying to imagine Dad, you know, out here, hiking around . . . "

Chris started laughing, then. "Oh, yeah, sure," he snorted. "Get real."

"He'd probably have to stash a cooler of beer every

mile or so along the trail to make it," I said, still chuckling.

Chris nodded. "And he'd be smoking and wheezing and coughing and stuff. It'd be really gross."

Jon didn't say anything. He just watched the two of us. I think he had some idea what was going on. I guess it wasn't real hard to figure out, actually.

We drifted along in silence for a while. Then Chris looked over his shoulder at me. I started to smile. He did, too. I started to laugh again. Chris joined me. In a matter of moments, we were both doubled over, our sides splitting.

"AAgghh!" Chris yelled, scaring a few birds away. "Can you just *see* it? I mean, it would be such a *trip* watching Dad trying to hack his way through the bushes . . . "

"He'd be laying big hawkers on trees and cussing at all the bugs," I said between howls of laughter.

"And complaining about how *hot* it is," Chris added.

"He'd be miserable," I said.

"Really awful," Chris said.

I paused for a second. "Maybe we should invite him out here," I said, half-serious.

"Yeah, like he'd come," Chris said.

"I guess you're right," I said. "It was just a thought."

"A crummy one," he said.

"But funny," I said. "You gotta admit it was funny."

"Just barely," Chris said, returning to his paddling viciously. I pitied the careless fish who wandered near Chris' side of the boat when he sliced his paddle into the water.

**When we returned to camp,** it was almost dinnertime. I was beat. It's hard to paddle a canoe upstream. My arms were aching, and I was sure I'd be stiff and sore the next morning.

Chris wasn't exactly looking chipper, either. But he had a happy, contented smile on his face. We hadn't seen a whole lot—except plenty of birds, reeds sticking up out of the water, and an occasional frog as it plopped away before us—but it had been fun.

Jon sat with all the other counselors at a separate table during dinner. Most of the counselors looked to be about Jon's age.

Chris and I slipped into the food line behind a tall, gangly kid who had glasses that seemed to be slipping off the end of his nose, a shirt that was half tucked in, and pea-green socks that absolutely did not match the rest of his clothes.

Because we'd gotten back from canoeing rather late, we were at the end of the line. I sure hoped there was food left by the time we got to where they were dishing out helpings onto plates. From where we stood, I couldn't see what we were having, but it smelled wonderful.

"What happens after dinner?" Chris whispered.

"Beats me," I whispered back. "This is all new to me."

"Tonight's marshmallow night," the tall, gangly kid in front of us said, half turning to face us.

"Marshmallow night?" asked Chris.

This kid nodded. The glasses almost came off his nose. Only a last minute save by his finger kept them from clattering to the floor. "Sure. We all sit around a big fire, roasting marshmallows. One of the counselors will probably play a guitar."

Chris groaned. "I'll bet we'll have to sing along, won't we?"

"If you know the words," this kid answered.

"How come you know so much about this stuff?" I asked him.

"I was here last year," he said, shrugging. "It's actually pretty fun. You'll like it."

"I doubt it," Chris said glumly.

"Where you from?" I asked the kid.

"D.C.," he said.

"So are we. Which part?"

"Fairfax County," he said, reappraising me with eyes that half-peered over the top of his glasses.

"Yeah, that's where we live, too. I go to Roosevelt. My name's Cally James. This is my brother, Chris. ' I thought about offering to shake his hand, but I jammed mine into my pocket instead.

"My name's Kent Volmerschmidt."

"Volmerschmidt?" I asked. "What kind of name's that?"

He grinned. As I'd half-expected, his teeth were green. They looked like they hadn't been brushed in about a hundred years. I could have sworn there was moss growing in there, somewhere. "It's German. It's gotta mean something, but I couldn't tell you what."

Chris piped up. "We're descendants of Jesse James," he offered.

"Really? That's pretty neat," said Kent.

"So where do you go to school?" I asked.

"Timothy Christian," Kent said.

"Where's that? I've never heard of it," I said.

"Most people haven't," he said. "It's a private, Christian school, K-to-12th, out in the country."

"Do ya like it?" I asked.

"It's okay, I guess," he said.

The line shifted forward. We shuffled forward with it. My stomach was really starting to growl. I wondered if I'd survive the wait in the line.

"Yikes, this line's slow," Chris said. "Why don't we just sort of wander up towards the front and cut in, like everybody always does at school?"

"How do you do that?" Kent asked, genuinely curious. I was certain Kent had never tried anything like that in his life.

"It's easy," Chris said. He glanced at the front of the line with an appraising eye. "First you grab a tray and your silverware. Then you hang back and watch the line right where they start serving the food. As soon as there's a break—like when a group's talking and they haven't quite gotten there yet—you bolt in front of them and put your tray out. Once they're serving you, nobody's gonna tell you to go back to the end."

I just shook my head. Chris could find a scam in just about anything. I wondered, briefly, how he was going to sit still long enough to hear people talk about the Bible over the next two weeks.

"Nah, I'll wait," Kent said. "I'm not *that* hungry."

Chris just shrugged. "Your loss."

Kids were already starting to leave the dining room by the time we finally got our food, but I didn't mind. I was so starved I was oblivious to what was going on around me. Chris wolfed his food down, too. Kent decided to join us. He just sort of picked at his food.

It was just starting to get dark outside when we'd finished. It was interesting, but it got dark a lot quicker in the mountains. The sun went "down" behind the hills a lot sooner.

There was already a small crowd gathered around one of the counselors at the huge campfire. He was playing a guitar, just as Kent had predicted. I started to drift over towards the fire.

Chris suddenly tugged on my shirtsleeve. "Come on," he said in a low whisper. "Let's bolt."

"Why?" I asked, perplexed. "Everybody's heading over to the fire."

"I don't feel like it," he said. "I'd rather do somethin' else instead. Nobody said we *have* to sit over there and eat marshmallows."

"Oh, come on, it'll be fun," I insisted.

"Yeah, sure, like a hole in the head," grumbled Chris.

I stood my ground. I wasn't letting him off the hook this easily. "Let's go. They're passing out the marshmallows now." I started to head over to the fire. Very reluctantly, Chris trudged along.

When we got there, the fire was just beginning to roar. The orange flames were already starting to cast long, deep shadows against the tree line.

Chris took a marshmallow and jammed it on the end of a stick. Hardly acknowledging anyone around him, he stuck it right in the heart of the fire.

The heat from the fire was intense. I stuck my marshmallow on the longest stick I could find and gingerly held it out at the edge of the fire. I glanced at Chris. He was still holding his marshmallow right in the heart of the fire.

When Chris finally pulled his free, it was black as

coal. I started to yell at him to let the thing cool before he took a bite, but I was a second too late.

"AAgghh!" he yelled as he bit into the black lump on the end of his stick.

"Blow on it," I called to him. "It'll cool."

"I think I burned my mouth," Chris said, gulping at the cool, night air that was starting to descend on us.

"You'll live."

"I doubt it," Chris answered. He took a second bite, more slowly this time. He pulled back again, because it was still too hot.

"You won't learn, will you?" I said, laughing.

"Nope," he said, giving me a cockeyed grin. "I just gotta live dangerously, you know."

My marshmallow had turned a nice, golden brown. I pulled it from the fire and blew on it to cool it down. I was just about to take a bite when Chris pointed off at something.

"What?" I asked.

"Look. There's something over there," he said.

I glanced away from the fire. No sooner had I turned my head than I felt a slight tug on the end of my stick. I jerked my head back around, but I was too late. My stick was empty. Chris was chewing away happily.

"Mmmm, boy, that's good," he said, *his* mouth full of *my* nice, golden-brown marshmallow.

"That was really crummy," I said.

"I know," Chris said. He offered me his own black marshmallow. "Here, you can have mine."

"No thanks," I snorted. I moved away from the fire and walked over to get another marshmallow. There was no doubt about it. Chris was something else.

When I returned, Chris was trying to peel off the black part of his marshmallow. "Man, just eat it," I said. "It won't kill you."

Chris didn't say anything. He just kept peeling until most of the black parts had flaked off onto the ground. Then, with a vicious grin, he pulled the gooey middle into his mouth.

"You should really try one," he said, chewing away. "These things are great."

Glaring at Chris, I stuck my white marshmallow into the fire, along with about fifty other kids. The campfire was really starting to fill up. I'd just started to munch away on my toasted marshmallow when one of the counselors stood up and asked for quiet.

I began to sit down near the fire when I noticed that Chris was starting to work his way back towards the edge of the crowd. I followed in his wake reluctantly, curious about what he had in mind.

Chris took a seat at the outer fringe of the crowd of kids, his back resting against a tree. "Better seat," he said when I arrived at his side.

"But you can't hear," I protested.

"Sure you can," he said.

I turned back towards the counselor. I could hear him, but just barely. "Chris, I'm moving in closer, where it's easier to hear," I told him.

"Go ahead. I'm fine right here."

I gave him a funny look. He sure was acting strangely, but I decided not to press it any further. I moved closer, took a seat on one of the many small logs that were sprinkled around the fire. I glanced back over my shoulder. Chris was leaning contentedly against the tree.

The speaker was one of the older counselors, a young man who looked to be in his 20s. He was definitely older than Jon, who was sitting just off to one side of him. My eye caught Jon's. He winked at me.

"Before we begin," the counselor was saying, "let's

say a prayer of thanks for today. I don't know about you, but my day was full of joy and wonder. God certainly has blessed us out here, right in the middle of His wonderful world."

We all bowed our heads. Before closing my eyes to pray, I glanced over at Chris. His head was bowed, too. *Good,* I thought. *At least I don't have to worry about that.*

"Dear Lord," the speaker began, "thank You for today. Thank You for giving all of us this time together, in the world You created. We know this isn't the wilderness, but thank You for the chance to listen to Your voice out here where there isn't much to get in the way.

"Lord, thank You for the fellowship and the friends. This is a special time together. Please help us to make the best of it. In Jesus' name. Amen."

I opened my eyes. I could feel the gentle, guiding touch of the Holy Spirit, directing my mind towards the words of the speaker. It amazed me, still, that God could actually enter my life that way.

"Okay," the speaker said, clapping his hands together. "Let's try a song, first. Maybe we can get Tim to play something we all know."

Most of the kids glanced expectantly at another counselor, who was sitting on a rock with the guitar balancing on one leg. The counselor, Tim, strummed a few chords. Some of the kids recognized it right away.

"It only takes a spark to get a fire going," a few of us sang. . . .

It was a time-honored campfire song. I'd never actually sung it around a campfire before, though. That made the song even nicer. When we'd finished, the first speaker stood up again.

As he began to speak again, I glanced over my

shoulder to see what Chris was doing.

He was gone. The spot where he'd been leaning against the tree was empty.

I looked over the knot of kids around me, trying to catch a glimpse of him. But I was pretty sure he'd just left. Most likely, he'd slipped away during the song, when no one was looking. I'd probably find him back at our cabin, reading or something.

"This isn't going to be easy," I muttered to no one in particular. "Not easy at all."

**They served breakfast at the crack of dawn.** And I mean the crack of dawn. At least breakfast was okay. The eggs and the biscuits were a little hard, but they weren't too bad, all things considered.

Chris and I sat with Kent Volmerschmidt and another kid, Rick Thompson. I'd met him the night before at the campfire. Rick was from Roanoke, like Jon. He was a wiry, feisty kid and had just a tad bit of wildness about him.

"Man, what Peter said last night was amazing," Kent said at one point during breakfast, his mouth still half full of eggs. Peter Simpson was the camp's chief counselor. "I couldn't stop thinkin' about it last night."

I glanced across the table at Chris, who wouldn't meet my gaze. He was staring intensely at his plate, picking at the food, moving it around a little to buy some time.

Just as I'd thought, I'd found him reading when I returned. He'd said something about being tired and about not *really* wanting to sit around some dumb, ol' campfire singing songs he didn't know.

But I knew better. He was still having a hard time with the Bible, even though Mom had talked to him about Jesus before. It made him uncomfortable, trying to think about all of it. He might not admit that, but I knew it was true.

So he just avoided the conversation at breakfast. I didn't let on to either Kent or Rick that he'd skipped the campfire talk and the songs.

"Yeah, it was purdy nice," Rick chipped in. "I liked what he had to say about thinkin' and speakin' like a child, and how you had to give up childish ways when you grow up."

"Which part of the Bible is that from?" Chris asked timidly. I looked at him in some surprise, because he'd guessed it was from the Bible and that he'd asked a question about it.

"Peter said it was from Corinthians," offered Kent. "And there's more from that part, about seeing God dimly through a mirror right now and that we won't see Him face-to-face or understand everything until after we die. . . . "

"Do you guys know everything that's in the Bible?" Chris asked.

"You kiddin'?" Rick said. "Who does?"

"I've read a lot of it," Kent said. "But I only remember some of the stories Jesus told."

Chris glanced at me. I met his gaze with a curious stare. "Nope, not me. I'm like Kent. I've read some and I remember some of the stories, but that's about it."

"Then how do you know it's all true, if you haven't read a lot of what's there?" he asked.

" 'Cause what I *have* read sounds purdy awwright to me," Rick said.

"It just makes sense," Kent said.

Again, Chris looked at me. I thought about a moment, forever trapped in my mind, when I'd hugged my mother on a bridge over a stream and finally admitted to myself that I did believe God existed, that the world had meaning and that I really did have a place in it.

Faith was the key. Without it, you had no hope of believing. I knew that.

Telling Chris this was another matter. "I guess I have faith that what Mom's always told me is right," I said finally. "That has a lot to do with it. I know she's read nearly all of the Bible, and I believe what she's taught me about it."

Chris nodded. I could see that he accepted that answer. It made a certain amount of sense to him. He trusted Mom, too.

But even with that kind of trust, it still required a colossal leap of faith to actually believe that Jesus would enter your life if you asked Him to, and He'd bring you near to God. There was no easy way to get to that point, and beyond.

Chris shifted gears abruptly. "Hey, anybody know what we're doin' today?" he asked generally.

"I heard tell we were takin' a hike through the woods this mornin'," Rick answered.

"I heard the same thing last night, from one of the counselors," Kent added. "There's about a seven-mile hike marked out through the woods around here."

"Great!" Chris said exuberantly. "Maybe we'll see a few bears."

"I'd settle for a few deer, if you don't mind," Kent said. "Bears are *mean.*"

"Yeah, you guys heard that old story, about two kids who were out campin' in the woods and heard a bear startin' to come towards their tent?" Rick asked. We all shook our heads.

"Well, one of the kids just started to sort of put his shoes on calmly, not really hurryin' or nuthin'. The other kid looked at him like he was crazy. 'There's a bear comin',' this second kid said. 'We better leave, if we're gonna outrun him.'

" 'I don't have to outrun the bear,' the first kid said as he finished tyin' his shoes. 'I just gotta outrun *you!*' "

*   *   *   *   *

They put counselors at both ends of the line when we started out on the hike, which was probably a pretty good idea.

Some of the kids started to fall behind almost right from the start. You could hear kids hollering all the way through the woods, in what seemed like all directions, because the path doubled back at points.

Chris and I stayed near the front of the pack through the hike. Actually, we stayed right at the very front. It wasn't hard to keep up with the counselors who were leading the group.

As we made our way through the woods, I began to notice that Chris was watching everyone around him like a hawk. He was taking in every word, every gesture, every exchange of glances.

It was easy to see what was happening to Chris, because much the same thing had happened to me not too long ago. Chris was hearing about a world he'd hardly heard about before and he was judging it, weighing it in the balance, trying to determine if it was real and true.

It was a hard choice, I knew. To believe in God you had to believe in something you couldn't see or talk to, at least not in the way Chris was used to.

Now that I was a Christian, I could "see" the way God acted in other people's lives—like in my mom, for instance. And I could "talk" to God indirectly by asking questions of Him and then getting answers in all sorts of different ways.

But you couldn't explain that to Chris, not right

now. He was looking for direct, concrete answers. He wanted to see God face-to-face, to wrestle with Him and ask Him all the questions that burned inside like white-hot coals.

As we began to work our way up a steep hill towards the end of the hike, I finally began to get a little winded. Not much, though. I was in pretty good shape, thanks to all the tennis I played. Chris wasn't breathing hard, either.

I could see the strain on a few faces, though, especially on some of the counselors who probably hadn't exercised a whole lot recently.

Chris slowed for just a second and let the rest of the pack we'd been walking with move on ahead up the steep incline. He leaned close. "A few of these guys are in lousy shape," he whispered.

"I noticed that," I whispered back.

We walked for a little bit more. "I've been listenin' to some of this stuff," he said finally.

"I've noticed that, too," I said.

Chris glanced at me sharply. The one person he hadn't been watching like a hawk was *me,* because I'd said almost nothing the entire hike. "Yeah, well, I don't buy hardly any of this," he pronounced with a scowl.

"Why's that?"

" 'Cause it's crazy, that's why."

"What's so crazy?"

Chris got a little animated. "Some of these counselors just wander around here and go on and on about all this stuff that God's told them, how they've learned all this really wonderful junk, and I *know* God hasn't actually talked to 'em or anything."

"I wondered if maybe you wouldn't think that," I said, smiling.

Glancing between the path and me, Chris asked, "Come on, Cally. God doesn't really *talk* to you, does He?"

"No, not really," I said honestly. "It doesn't work like that."

"So how's it work?"

A broad, mottled leaf drifted lazily to the ground just in front of us. An idea came to me. I picked up the leaf and handed it to Chris. "See this leaf?" I asked him. He nodded. "Tell me what made it break free of the tree and then fall to the ground."

Chris thought for a moment. "A squirrel probably ran across the branch and knocked it loose. Then it fell."

"Did you see the squirrel run across the branch?"

"No," he said, giving me a strange look.

"But it seems like a pretty good idea, that it might have happened that way even though you didn't actually see it happen that way?"

"Well, sure.'

"Actually, have you *ever* seen a squirrel run across a branch and knock a leaf loose?"

Chris thought about it for a moment. "I guess not," he said. "But I know it can happen. It just makes sense."

"Sure it does," I agreed. "Now, once the leaf's been knocked loose, what makes it fall to the ground?"

"I don't know. It just comes down."

"Why doesn't it just hang there in the air?"

"Oh, you know, like that guy Newton and the apple, the gravity pulls it down to the earth."

"Gravity pulls it down? That's what makes the leaf fall to the ground?"

Chris glanced at the leaf he was holding in his hand; or, to be more precise, that he was beginning to crumple in his hand. "That's right, gravity."

"You've actually *seen* gravity? You know what it is?"

"Give me a break, would ya? Nobody's actually seen gravity."

"You just know it works, because you see leaves fall to the ground and balls come back down after they're tossed up in the air, right?"

"Yeah, right."

"It's just exactly like that with God," I said with a crispness that surprised me. "You can't see God. You only see the results of what He does in the world."

We came to the top of the hill. I could just barely see the outline of the camp through the leaves. A few of the kids began to sprint towards camp. Chris and I held back. He was thinking.

"Sometimes it makes sense," he said.

"I know."

"And sometimes it doesn't," he added quickly.

"I know that, too."

There are so many things to believe or follow in the world. In fact, there are zillions of things coming at you all the time, from every direction. It's hard to sort through what means anything and what is just an accident.

If I spend just an hour in front of the television, I am bombarded with so many different messages it's hard to pick one that's really and truly important. Sometimes it's easier to just ignore all of them.

If I walk through the halls at school and listen to the babble of voices of all the kids, I could get lost in all the different conversations. Sometimes it's easier just to block all of them out and keep moving.

When you go to a party, it can drive you crazy trying to pay attention to what everyone is doing and saying. It's a lot simpler to just pick one corner of the room and pretend everything else doesn't exist.

I wondered how often Chris had been alone with his thoughts. Probably not very often. He always had friends around, or he sought them out. He almost never drifted off somewhere by himself. He always wanted to be at the center of every storm.

Out here, at least when we were in the woods, it was a little different, a little slower. There weren't quite as many ideas and notions bombarding us.

"Let's go," I said to him. "I'll race you back to camp."

Chris took off without a word. I had to really push it to beat him. Somewhere along the line, Chris had gotten almost as fast as me. Even though he was two years younger than me, it wouldn't be long before he was neck and neck with me in just about everything. It was a scary thought.

**Chris was waving the hammer around** like a madman, practically blue in the face with anger. It was all I could do to keep him from heaving the thing deep into the forest.

Chris really had no right to be so angry, but I could understand it. I'd be mad, too, if they'd sent me out to gather firewood with just a hammer. A hammer? What were you supposed to do with *that*?

"He's crazy!" he fumed at me as we wandered through the darkening forest. "Stark, raving crazy."

"Chris, just calm down."

"*Don't* tell me to calm down," he snapped. "I don't want to calm down. I want to take this hammer and—"

"No, you don't," I said. "Trust me. You'd regret it later."

"Maybe," he said with a tight, vicious grin. "But I'd sure have fun right now."

It had been an accident, really. Chris would never intentionally harm anyone. It had been an accident. That's all. Just an accident.

Yes, it was true, Chris had been doing something he wasn't supposed to. But he hadn't meant to hurt anyone. But that didn't sway the chief counselor. Chris had broken the rules, someone had gotten hurt, and now he was taking his lumps.

After we'd gotten back from the hike, we'd all eaten a big lunch and then fooled around for a little that afternoon. Chris and I had gone out to the stables and ridden a couple of horses.

I mean, we *tried* to ride the horses. It's a whole lot harder than it looks, believe me. The dumb animals don't do anything you tell them. Or, rather, they do whatever they feel like, despite what you're yelling at them.

It about drove me insane. No matter what I tried, the horse they gave me seemed to do just exactly the opposite. If I clucked on the reins to make it go faster, the dumb horse slowed. If I kicked in my heels to make it slow down, the horse sped up.

Finally, it began to dawn on me that I wasn't talking in horse language. It was programmed to do something on command. You just had to figure out what the commands were.

The reins didn't make it go, I finally discovered, they made the horse stop or slow down. And prods from parts of my anatomy always made it speed up, not the other way around. Oh well. I guess I wasn't cut out as a great horseman.

It was just as well. My backside was so sore by the time we'd finished that I almost couldn't sit down. Not that I told anyone this. But it did make it a little tough to walk without a limp.

Just before dinner, the counselors had gathered all the kids together by the campfire and passed out hand axes, long axes, and saws.

"Now, remember, we just need firewood. Don't go chopping down the forest," Peter told us in his sternest voice.

"What's that mean?" one of the other kids asked.

"It means," Peter answered patiently, "that you

should *not* chop down anything that's still alive. Don't chop away at any live trees. Just cut up trees that have already fallen, or big branches. Is that clear?"

Everyone nodded and then faded into the forest. Chris had been given one of the long axes and he slung it over his shoulder proudly, fancying himself a lumberjack, no doubt.

I had a saw, which wasn't a whole lot of fun. Rick and Kent came along with us. They both had small hand axes.

There were kids in every direction, hacking away at branches and fallen limbs. I picked out a likely target—a large tree that had obviously been struck by lightning because it had toppled over and the top was missing—but Chris insisted we go deeper into the forest.

We all grumbled, but followed. For some reason, the fact that Chris was carrying the long ax somehow made him the team leader. Sensing this, he swaggered through the forest.

"This is it," he announced a few minutes later, after we were well into the woods. I could only just hear the muffled yells of the other kids. There really wasn't anyone else around except the four of us.

"This is what?" I asked Chris. There wasn't any dead wood around anywhere that I could see.

"Yeah, what ya talkin' about, Chris?" asked Rick, his hand ax drooping by his side.

"This," Chris said grandly, pointing at a sapling that had not yet grown as tall as the other trees surrounding it. "I'll chop it down with my ax, then you guys can cut it up into firewood."

"Peter said we weren't supposed to chop down live trees," Kent said quietly.

"Aw, what does he know?" Chris grumbled, slightly

annoyed. "This will burn a whole lot better when we bring it back. It'll be the best wood in the camp."

I started to tell Chris that green wood won't burn, but Kent spoke first. "But Peter said—"

"I don't *care* what Peter said, or what he didn't say!" Chris almost yelled. "I'm chopping this tree down. Is anyone going to help me when I'm finished, or do I have to do the whole thing myself?"

Kent and Rick both glanced at me. I took a deep breath, not quite sure what to do. I never knew what to do when Chris got bull-headed like this. Once he'd made up his mind, there was no turning back. He forged ahead, no matter what the consequences.

"Chris, why don't we go back to that tree that I spotted?" I said in the most reasonable voice I could muster.

"No!" Chris said. "I'm takin' this tree back with me. Are you with me, or not?"

"Come on, Chris," I pleaded, "the counselor told us that we had to go find dead wood to chop. Let's just do that, all right?"

Chris just glared at the three of us. Kent and Rick were going to follow my lead. I was pretty sure of that. But there was no way I could stop Chris now.

"So are you with me, or not?" Chris asked as he took the ax off his shoulder and held it in the ready position.

"We're going to find some dead wood, Chris," I answered. "I wish you'd come with us."

His answer was a swift, vicious swing at the base of the sapling. There was a resounding "thunk" as the sharp ax bit into the young tree. Chris jerked at the ax, pulled it free, and swung it at the tree a second time.

"Come on," I said to the other two. "Let's leave him alone."

We moved off about twenty feet or so, to where Rick
had seen a large limb that had fallen to the ground
from one of the large trees that stood all around us.

We all got to work breaking the limb up into firewood. I took the bigger sections with my saw. They
chopped up some of the smaller parts into kindling.
Every so often, we all glanced up to see how Chris
was doing.

He was certainly attacking the sapling with a ven-
geance. The *thunks* had turned to *thwacks* as he'd
gotten into the heart of the tree. We could see little
bits of wood fly off with every swing.

"Man, he sure is stubborn," Rick said.

"You can say that again," Kent added. "When he
makes up his mind, there's no turnin' back."

I didn't say anything. I wasn't sure I could defend
Chris just now. What he was doing was just flat-out
wrong, and I was pretty sure he knew it, too. But they
were right. He sure was stubborn.

It happened just as Chris was beginning to topple
the tree. Knowing he had only a few more blows to go,
Chris was swinging the ax as hard as he possibly
could.

It was on one of those swings that the head of the
ax came free. Chris swung from his heels towards the
sky and the blade just slipped right off the top of the
handle. It hurtled through the air, straight at the three
of us.

I was looking up when it happened, so I saw the
whole thing. I watched in fascinated horror. It happened so slowly, like someone was taking snapshots
of each sequence.

The blade arced high in the air, knifed through some
leaves, hit a branch, and started spinning wildly as it
began to descend. I could see that the blade was still

falling roughly in our direction.

"Hit the ground!" I yelled at the top of my lungs an instant or two before the blade fell from the sky. Kent and Rick reacted almost instantly, covering their heads.

I covered mine, too, and dove for the ground. I never heard the blade land, but I didn't have to. An instant after it hit, Rick began to howl with pain.

"It hit me! It hit me!" Rick was yelling, holding the side of his head. Kent and I both rushed to his side. I could hear Chris crashing through the forest undergrowth.

Thankfully, I couldn't see any blood between Rick's fingers. And he hadn't passed out or anything, so I didn't think he was hurt badly.

"Let me see," I said to Rick, trying to peer through his hand.

"It hurts like crazy," he said, still holding his head and refusing to let go.

"I'll bet it does," I said, gently taking his hand and moving it aside. There was a tiny gash on the side of his head, and not much blood to speak of. Rick was very, very lucky. It looked as if the blunt end of the ax head had just grazed him.

Chris almost crashed into us when he arrived an instant later. "I didn't mean to. It was an accident, really," he said, gasping for air.

"It's all right, Chris, he isn't hurt badly," I said.

"It was just an accident. It slipped off . . . "

"He's okay," I said in a sterner voice.

Chris peered over my shoulder, trying to see what had happened to Rick. The gash in his head still hadn't started to bleed much, but I could see that he was going to have a nasty lump on his head for a little bit.

"Let's go back to camp," I said to Rick. "I'll help you."

Rick got to his feet. He was a little unsteady, but seemed to be able to walk without much help. Still, I draped one of his arms over my shoulder.

Chris didn't say anything on the way back. He retrieved the blade, which had little flecks of blood on it, and then hung back a little as we walked through the forest. I couldn't blame him. I was sure he felt just sick inside about the freak accident.

When we got back to camp, one of the counselors took Rick inside the administration building to the nurse's quarters, where they examined him more closely. As it turned out, Rick was just fine. He would have a lump, for sure, but he was all right.

Chris and I, though, wouldn't hear about this until later. Peter Simpson took us off to the side shortly after we'd arrived. He was so angry I could see the veins on the side of his neck.

"You should have known better, young man," he said to me.

I almost started to protest. Me? What had I done? It was my dumb brother who'd been mule-headed, I wanted to protest. There was no way I could have stopped Chris. But I said nothing, realizing that it was futile.

"And you," Peter said, turning his awful gaze on Chris, "what can you possibly have to say for yourself?"

"I . . . I didn't mean to," he stammered.

"I'm quite sure you didn't, but that's hardly an excuse," Peter said. "You were expressly told not to cut down any live trees, yet you did so anyway. Why?"

Chris looked like he was in pain. "I dunno. I just wanted to, I guess."

"You just wanted to?"

"Yeah, it seemed like the right thing to do, I guess."

"The right thing to do?"

"Maybe not the right thing," Chris said, backtracking quickly. "But I had this really great ax, you see, and I wanted to use it and it wouldn't have been the same trying to chop up some crummy tree that had already fallen to the ground . . . "

"I see," Peter said sharply. "So you just decided to take matters into your own hands."

"Well, yeah, I guess," he said morosely.

"And do you regret that decision, now?" Peter asked, more gently.

I could see the anger flare up again briefly in Chris' eyes. "I was almost through the tree," he said, not meeting Peter's gaze. "If that dumb blade hadn't come off . . . "

Peter pursed his lips in anger. It was clear to both of us that the only thing Chris regretted was the accident, not his poor judgment in the first place.

"I think you need to go back into the forest," Peter said after a very long silence that seemed to last for an eternity. "And this time, I think maybe you should take a different tool with you."

Peter walked away, then, and disappeared into one of the buildings next to the administration building. He reemerged a moment later carrying a hammer. He handed the hammer to Chris, who just stared at it blankly.

"What am I supposed to do with *this?*" asked Chris.

"Bring back some firewood," Peter said.

"With a hammer?"

"Use your imagination," Peter said tersely.

Chris continued to stare at the hammer. He was clearly incredulous. This made no sense to him. For that matter, it made no sense to me. But I was willing to go along. Anything to get away from Peter's terrible gaze.

"Let's go, Chris," I said, pulling on my brother's arm.

Chris looked at me, then at Peter, and then shrugged with resignation. He followed my lead and trailed behind me as we wandered back into the forest. Peter watched us go.

"That guy's a nut case," Chris said under his breath when we were well away from the chief counselor.

"Chris, what you did was wrong," I said.

"You takin' his side?"

"No," I said quickly. "I'm just sayin' that what you did was wrong, that's all."

"Don't you think I know that?" he snapped.

"Do you?"

" 'Course I do. Who wouldn't?"

We started to move into the forest. Chris just swatted branches away angrily with the hammer. Some of them rebounded into my face.

We hadn't gone very far when Chris stopped dead in his tracks and started to wave his hammer around, raving like a madman. Like I said, I couldn't blame him for his anger. But it really was directed at the wrong person. Peter wasn't to blame; Chris was.

But there was no telling him that right now. He'd have to sort it all out on his own, over time.

"I'll teach him," Chris fumed.

"You'll what?"

"You'll see," he answered, moving off into the forest again. He was now clearly stalking something.

He spotted what he was looking for a minute later. This time, it was a very young tree, only just out of the ground. It was only slightly taller than Chris.

Before I could stop him, Chris knelt on the ground at the base of this tiny tree and began to hammer away. And he was banging away with the blunt end of the hammer, not the claw.

"Are you crazy?" I asked him. "What's that supposed to accomplish?"

*Whack!* went the hammer. "He wanted firewood," Chris said. *Whack!* "Well, that's what he's getting." *Whack!* "Starting with this tree."

"It'll take you forever," I protested. "And it's a live tree, not a dead one."

"I don't care," growled Chris. "He wanted firewood. He's gettin' firewood."

I stared numbly at my half-crazed brother. He was flailing away at the tree in pure, blind anger. What's more, he was actually managing to knock the tree down. As unlikely as it seemed, the tree was beginning to break under the steady blows from the hammer.

In a matter of minutes, the job was done. With a savagery I'd never seen before in Chris, he rained blow after blow on that poor, hapless tree until, with a crack, it snapped at the base and teetered to the side. A few more vicious bashes and Chris had felled the tree.

"There," he said. "Let's see what he does with *that.*"

I just shook my head sadly. It would make lousy firewood. The tree was very green. In fact, it was so green it might not even burn. But I guess that wasn't the point. It wasn't the tree that was burning right now. No, something else was, right before my eyes.

**Our third day at camp began** much like the previous day. There was nothing extraordinarily special or ominous about it.

The eggs and orange juice were lousy like they had been the day before. And it was still hard to keep my eyes open through breakfast.

We had a long day in front of us. The counselors had organized a day-long trip in the canoes. We were piling the canoes on top of the cars, driving to a river that came out of Mount Argus, and then making our way down it.

Fortunately, we wouldn't have to paddle back. Some of the counselors would meet us downriver and we'd load the canoes and drive back to camp.

Including counselors, we would ride three to a canoe. There weren't enough counselors to go around, however, so we wouldn't have one in ours. That was just fine and dandy with Chris, who was still smoldering over the "hammer incident."

Kent and Rick, who'd long since forgiven Chris, planned to ride in their own canoe. Jon was going to join them, and he vowed to keep a close eye on us.

It was a little chilly that morning, so I decided to wear a windbreaker until it warmed up. Chris told me I was crazy. I thought he was the one who was crazy. He just wore a T-shirt. I could see the goose pimples on his arms, which he kept rubbing vigorously.

"You'll roast when it warms up," reasoned Chris.

"So I take the windbreaker off," I answered. "Big deal."

"But then you'll have to cart it around with you."

"We'll be in a canoe, you nincompoop."

"Yeah, but you'll have to sit on it, or tie it around your waist, or put it under your feet or something," Chris said, refusing to yield.

I just shook my head. There were times when it didn't pay to try to reason with Chris. This was one of those times.

We headed out in the cars just as the sun broke over the top of Mount Argus. It disappeared, briefly, as we drove towards the mountain, though.

It took us half an hour or so to make the drive around Mount Argus and then find a point along the river where we could launch our canoes. I wasn't really paying any attention at all to where we were or where we were going. I figured the counselors knew what they were doing.

I did happen to notice, though, that we drove well up the mountain before we parked the cars. That meant the first part of the trip, at least, would be downhill.

Chris volunteered to steer, which was fine with me. I donned my life preserver, secured the lunch they'd packed for us beneath my seat at the front, and hopped in after Chris had eased the canoe into the water.

Chris pushed us away from the shore and we joined the other canoes that were drifting lazily down the river.

"As much as possible," Peter Simpson yelled when we were all in the river, "I want us to stick together.

Don't attempt anything foolish. Try to avoid rocks and hidden logs. And if your canoe turns over, don't panic. Float beside it until another canoe can help you right it."

"What if we get attacked by bears?" someone called out.

Peter smiled. "Don't worry, you won't be. Now, let's move out."

It was nice that we were going downriver. "I wouldn't want to paddle back up this river," I said over my shoulder as we started off.

"That's for sure," answered Chris.

The river was pretty wide at this point, so it wasn't too difficult for the group to stay bunched together. As we moved further down the mountain, though, it began to narrow and the group of canoes began to string out along the river.

Chris and I weren't in any particular hurry. With the current doing most of our work for us, we hung towards the back of the group and watched the shoreline as we drifted past. At one point, we told Jon that we'd catch up right away. Not to worry.

I spotted a couple of raccoons, a possum family, a whole bunch of squirrels, some really ugly crows, a muskrat before it vanished into a hole in the bank, and one very skittish deer.

I glanced over my shoulder at one point. Chris was just staring off into space, his paddle trailing in the water. I felt much the same as he did. Neither of us seemed to have any energy to put into this trip.

Finally, though, when we'd drifted well behind the rest of the group, I decided we'd better pour on at least a little coal and fire the engines.

"Let's roll, dude," I called out. "We're way behind everybody else. I can't even see them now."

"So? We can always catch them, if we have to."

"I know, but let's at least catch up a little."

With a deep sigh, Chris dipped his oar in the water and began to paddle. As our canoe leaped forward just slightly, it caused a slight ripple. It was then that I noticed the current was beginning to pick up.

We began to move faster as Chris and I worked our oars together. Stroke, lift, dip. The canoe started to cut through the water with some authority. We'd drifted quite a ways behind the group, though, because no one was in sight after nearly five minutes of steady paddling.

As we began to make our way down a huge bend in the river, Chris started to steer us towards a side canal that seemed to make a shortcut through the bend.

"Where are you going?" I asked him.

"We'll head 'em off at the pass," Chris said.

"You don't know this will take us back to the main river," I warned.

"Ah, sure it will," he said. "Don't worry."

"I'm not. I just don't want to get lost."

"We won't. Paddle."

I returned to my task silently, still concerned. But the canal seemed harmless. If anything, the water was calmer here than the main river. And it did appear to cut through in a straight line.

Within minutes, though, it changed. The canal began to move off to the right, away from the main river. And the current began to pick up.

"Maybe we should try to go back," I said finally.

"No way," Chris answered. "I'm not paddling back up that river."

"But what if we . . . "

"We won't!" Chris said sharply. "This will join up. It has to."

The current was strong enough here that I could see a few foam caps as the water swirled around us on either side. Our canoe was moving along at a pretty good clip, now.

I heard the rumbling first. It was clearly coming from somewhere downriver. When I pointed this out to Chris, he just shrugged.

"We'll see," he said grimly, and continued paddling.

The rumbling quickly turned to a dull roar and, at last, into a full-throated battle cry as our little side canal began to turn into rapids that continued around a sharp bend a few hundred feet away.

"Steer us to the bank," I ordered.

Chris complied without a word. When we'd reached the bank, I hopped out and pulled the nose of the canoe onto the shore. Chris sat at the back, not moving.

"What are we gonna do now?" he asked quietly.

"*You* got us into this mess," I said.

"Come on, Cally, I mean it," he pleaded. "What are we gonna do?"

I sighed. "I don't know. I suppose we could go on and see if we can sort of navigate through those rapids. Or we can try to carry the canoe back to the river through the forest."

Chris and I both glanced at the rapids together, instinctively. We both made the same decision, at almost the same time.

"Let's try it," I said. "But let's trade places, first." Chris laid his oar down at the back of the canoe without a word and began to climb out of the canoe. When he was standing on the bank, I moved to the back of the canoe and picked up the oar. Chris scrambled in and I shoved off.

When we hit the first wave of the rapids, I let the

canoe drift up and over without trying to steer it too much. My one aim was to keep the canoe as straight as possible. I didn't want it turning sideways, where it could capsize.

It soon got much trickier, though; especially when we began to make the turn around the bend. There was white foam everywhere. The roar of the rapids was loud enough that I couldn't hear what Chris said if he didn't turn around to look at me, which he obviously wasn't going to do.

The canoe lurched over an especially swift rapid. The front of the canoe dipped precariously into the water, spraying water into Chris' face. I thrust my paddle deep into the water to steady the canoe as we continued to move swiftly down the river.

We almost shot over the next rapid. I tried as hard as I could to slow the canoe down, but there was no slowing it down now. The best I could hope for was to keep it straight and hope the rapids ended soon.

Faster and faster we raced. The front of the canoe plunked deep into the water again, spilling water into the canoe, which then sloshed around our feet.

"We're gonna make it!" I heard Chris cry out. I looked up from my task. There was calm water just ahead, not more than a hundred feet or so in front of us. But we had the heaviest part of the rapids yet to negotiate before we reached it.

And just before the calm water, the rapids seemed to drop off. I had no idea what they dropped off *into.*

One, two, three, four. With the passage of each succeeding rapid, we picked up even more speed. As we began to approach the drop-off, we were moving so fast it was all I could do to keep my oar in the water to steer. The water was battering us hard. My right hand was starting to get numb.

Chris and I both started to yell as we careened into the drop-off. The canoe surged up and over the last rapid, and dropped quickly. The boat began to tip sideways.

It dropped a good four or five feet and crashed hard onto some jagged rocks. The jolt when we hit threw me forward. I slammed my head against the side of the canoe.

The canoe almost went over, but righted itself at the last instant. I looked at Chris, slightly dizzy. My head was throbbing. Chris was holding his right arm. He'd probably banged it against the side of the boat.

Then I noticed the water. It was pouring into the canoe. And I mean pouring. In buckets. There was a huge, gaping hole right in the middle of the canoe. I could see the splinters all around the edge of the hole where a jagged rock had obviously smashed through.

Despite the pain in my head, I began to paddle furiously for the shoreline off to our right. It would only be a matter of minutes before we were swamped. Chris glanced behind him, saw the hole and the water rushing through, and began to paddle madly as well.

By the time we'd reached shore, the boat was nearly half full of water. Chris climbed wearily from the canoe and pulled it ashore. I clambered out right behind him, grabbed the canoe, rolled it over to empty out the water, and then let it rest on the shore.

We both collapsed in a heap on the shore. We lay there for a few minutes before I finally struggled to my feet to inspect the damage.

It was hopeless. The hole was huge, at least a couple of feet across. There was no way to repair it, not out here in the middle of nowhere. We'd have to walk from here. And it would be a *long* walk.

**"So what do we do now?"**

There was no fear in Chris' voice. Just a weariness, and maybe a little anger at himself for choosing such a "shortcut."

"We walk, kid," I said, still refusing to believe that we'd just put a two-foot hole in the bottom of our canoe. Yet there was the hole, staring up at the azure sky.

"But where do we walk to?" asked Chris. "We'll never catch up to the rest of the group. No way."

"Yeah, I guess you're right. They're going downriver and they're probably miles away by now."

"So we'll have to walk back the way we came?"

I glanced back up the river, but I couldn't see much because of the thick stand of trees surrounding us. "Got to, I guess. We probably ought to go over the top of Mount Argus and work our way down the other side towards camp."

"Do we *have* to climb that mountain?" pleaded Chris.

"It might take us forever to walk around it," I laughed. "Might as well go over the top. It's easier."

Chris sighed. "Ouch."

I thought about our predicament for a little bit. Even though it had warmed up some, it would start to get very chilly by the end of the day. If we had to walk all the way back, I knew we wouldn't make it back to camp by the end of the day.

Which meant that we'd have to find someplace to camp that night, someplace warm. Where that might be was anyone's guess.

"We'd better get going, Chris. It's a long way back," I said, pulling myself upright slowly. My head was still throbbing. Most likely I would have quite a lump from where I'd cracked my head on the canoe.

We left the canoe where it was, the nose pulled up onto the shore. There didn't seem much point in pulling it all the way up or doing anything else with it. The canoe was wrecked pretty good. We both tossed our lifejackets inside it. We wouldn't be needing them now.

Fortunately, we hadn't lost our lunch. It was real soggy, but still intact. I took the sandwich, crackers, and apple from my bag and stuffed them into the pockets of my windbreaker. Chris had to carry his bag as it was. He didn't have a windbreaker.

We began the long trek in silence. There wasn't much to say, actually. Chris knew he'd made a mistake. There was no point talking about it. The mistake wouldn't go away. I knew he felt bad about it. One look at his face told me that.

As we walked, I tried to calculate how far back it was to camp. We'd been in the canoe for at least an hour, maybe more. That meant we probably had at least ten miles before us just to get to Mount Argus. It had taken us half an hour to go around the mountain by car, so we probably had another few miles to go up and over the mountain to get to camp.

But I also figured that we'd never actually make it back to the mountain. Once they discovered that we were missing from the canoe group, they'd come looking for us. There were places along the river they could wait for us, which is what I thought they'd do. Most likely, we'd be riding back to camp tonight in someone's car.

Then again, that might just be wishful thinking. It was possible they wouldn't wait for us along the river and we'd have to walk all the way back. *No, they'd come get us.* I was sure of that.

It was very slow going. It's funny. When you're drifting alongside the shore in a canoe, the untamed forest always looks like it would be easy to walk through. Now that we were actually here, walking in the deep forest, it seemed like a jungle.

There were dead trees and vines and thick grass and all sorts of things to slow you down as you moved along. I was spending as much time going around things as I was walking up the river.

"Hey, Cally," Chris said, slightly winded, after we'd been walking for a good forty-five minutes or so.

"Yeah, what?" I was in no mood for casual conversation. I'd scraped my ankle on a protruding stick a while back, and it stung like crazy. On top of that, I was sure a mosquito had gotten me on the back of my neck, because I felt compelled to scratch it every few seconds.

"I was just thinkin'."

"That's a change," I snapped.

"Come on, I'm bein' serious."

"Okay, what already?"

"Well, I was just sort of wonderin' how mad you are at me," Chris said. There was just a tiny trace of remorse in his voice.

"I'm not *nearly* as mad at you as Peter Simpson's gonna be," I snorted.

"Aw, I don't care about him," Chris scowled. "A

few days, I won't ever see him again."

I stubbed my toe on a rock. "Ouch! And you'll see me for the rest of your life? That it?"

"Somethin' like that."

"What if I said this was about the dumbest thing you've ever done and that I'd be mad at you for the rest of your life?"

Chris stopped in his tracks. "You're not really—"

I plucked a dead branch from a nearby tree and, without pausing, flipped it behind me at Chris. He ducked, and it just barely missed him. "Oh, give me a break," I said. " 'Course I'm not that mad at you. Anybody could have made the same mistake."

"I mean, there was no way I'd have gone that way if I'd known about all that rough water," Chris said.

"Chris, I *know* that."

"So you're really not all that mad at me?"

I stopped and turned around to look at him. I cocked my head off to one side, giving Chris a curious, sidelong glance. "Look, you numbskull, how many times do I have to say it. I'm not mad."

"I'm just checkin', that's all," Chris said mildly.

"Well, stop it. If you don't, then I will get mad." I whirled, then, and began to plow through the undergrowth again.

"Hey, Cally," Chris said a few moments later.

"What!" I yelled, slightly exasperated. My voice seemed to disappear into the trees. I was surprised it didn't carry further than it did.

"How 'bout God? D'ya think He's pretty steamed at me? I mean, about how I am sometimes?"

I couldn't help it. I broke into a huge grin. Chris couldn't see it, of course, because I was facing away from him. But it just struck me. Chris could sure be funny about things, sometimes.

"Probably so," I answered.

"So what am I supposed to do about that, assumin' that God really exists? And I'm not sayin' He does, course, but just assumin' that He does and that He's really boiled right now?"

I could tell it made Chris nervous, talking about God. I couldn't blame him, though. God made everybody nervous, me included. Just thinking about the possibilities made most people nervous.

"Between you and Him, Chris," I said without looking back. "You gotta settle the score with Him, not me. I can't help you there."

"But how do I actually *do* that?"

I thought about my own life for a second. Whenever I did a sin, especially a real whopper, I always tried to tell God I was real, real sorry. And it never seemed to quite work. I mean, I was so crummy and God was so perfect, so distant from me. It just didn't seem to work.

I'd walk around for days, telling God I was sorry over and over and over. Like the time I got in a fight and was kicked out of school and off the tennis team. I tried telling God I was sorry. I really did. But it just wouldn't work. It was as if God wouldn't listen.

But then I remembered there was Jesus. I knew He'd listen. He'd been through it before, when He was a man. I could ask Jesus to help me, to stand between God's anger and me and say I was real, real sorry for what I'd done.

As soon as I'd done that, I knew it worked. God the Father would listen to Jesus. I knew He'd listen to His own Son. And as quickly as I asked Jesus to help, the Holy Spirit would tell me that God had heard my prayer.

"It's not easy, Chris," I said finally. "But you have to

sort of ask Jesus to help you. When you're really sorry
for something, Jesus can help you tell God about it."

"Why do you need Jesus?"

"Can you imagine what God is like, what He looks
like?"

"No, I guess not."

"Can you imagine how you'd tell Him you're sorry?"

"I'd just say it, that's all."

"And you'd be sure God would hear you?"

"I dunno," Chris said. "I hope so."

"But you *can* imagine Jesus? You can see what He
might look like, because He was a human just like you
and me?"

"Sure, of course."

A picture of a big, huge castle, surrounded by rivers
and moats and patrolled by fire-breathing dragons,
suddenly burst into my mind. "Think of it this way," I
said. "Imagine that God's the king and that He lives in
this monstrous castle, which you can't really get to."

"Okay."

"You stand outside, looking in, wondering what it's
like inside and what the king looks like. But you can't
really go inside because you don't belong there. Only
certain people are allowed inside, and you're not one
of them."

"If you say so."

"So you stand outside, yelling at the guards to let
you in so you can see the king. Then out comes this
guy, who's the king's son. He stands there and listens
to your story. Then he takes it inside and tells the king
all about it."

"I don't think it's really like that," Chris said. I could
hear the frown in his voice.

"I said it was *something* like that," I said defensively.

Chris sighed. "Okay, I think I get it, sort of. I gotta tell Him I'm sorry."

"If you are."

"Yeah, I'm sorry. I really am."

I was already beginning to cramp up a little, and we were only a few miles into our trek back to camp. I was certain Chris would be very, very sorry by the time we got back to camp, at the rate we were going.

"Well?" I asked after a few seconds of silence.

"Well, what?" Chris fired right back.

"What are you gonna do?"

" 'Bout what?" he asked.

Chris could drive you crazy. Absolutely, stark-raving, bonkers crazy. "What we were just *talking* about," I said.

"Oh, that."

"Yeah, that," I snapped. "So what're you gonna do about it?"

"Oh, I dunno," Chris mused. "I guess I'll think about it a little. It sort of makes sense."

Like I said, Chris can drive you crazy, if you let him. The trick is not letting him get to you. It's too bad I've never quite learned how to just completely, totally ignore him. Life would be easier, if I could just learn that one trick.

# 10

**We probably should have saved our lunch,** but
Chris was starving right around noon. So was I. We'd
put in a good number of miles — although the mountain
wasn't anywhere in sight — and I still thought the
group would catch up to us by the end of the day.

So we sat down on the river bank and ate our
lunches; they had dried out some during the walk.
Neither of us thought much about what we might do
in a day or two if we were still walking home. A day
or two seemed like forever.

My legs didn't hurt too much right now, but I could
tell they'd be real stiff tomorrow. Even though I was in
pretty good shape, I was asking them to go above and
beyond the call of duty right now.

"Let's go," I said, shaking away the cobwebs. Both
of us had been sitting there, staring out at the river.
Neither of us felt much like going on, but we had to.
There was no choice, really.

"All right," sighed Chris, picking himself off the
ground wearily.

Hours later, the mountain still wasn't in sight, however. I was sure we'd walked at least ten miles, but
we were still walking on level ground beside the river.
I was beginning to wonder how long it would, in fact,
take us to get back to camp if they didn't find us first.

By dinnertime, my stomach was ready for some food

again. There was only one, slight problem. There was none around. We'd even left our apple cores and the bag behind. Which meant we'd just have to go without for tonight.

I glanced over my shoulder. The sun was just starting to sink beneath the hills to the west. In an hour or so, it would disappear. Darkness would fall very quickly after that. It was time to find somewhere to spend the night.

"Hey, Chris, let's get a drink then move away from the river," I said, stopping.

"Why, what's up?"

"We should find a place to spend the night," I said.

"Why can't we just stay along the river?"

I vaguely remembered something about how cold it can get along a riverbank at night, even during the summer. I also remembered that animals, like mountain lions and bears, come to the banks of a river to drink during the darkness.

"I think it would be safer if we moved away from the river," I said.

Chris shrugged, and turned away without a word. We began to work our way north, away from the river.

We walked for a half hour or so until there was no longer a slight dampness beneath our feet. I kept my eyes peeled for a good place to stay during the night.

It was interesting, but I could feel the temperature start to drop almost the instant the sun disappeared behind the hills, and darkness started to move in quickly.

It's strange the way you don't notice things until you have to. When you're in camp and the sun starts to go down, you walk back to your cabin and grab a sweater without thinking about it.

But there was no cabin room in which to grab an

extra sweater out here. And there was no bed with
nice, fluffy covers to keep you warm as the night air
became very chilly . . .

Chris and I both heard the sound at the same time,
because we both glanced back over our shoulders almost the same instant. We both heard the distinct
*whop, whop, whop* before we saw lights through the
leaves of the trees.

"A helicopter," I said.

"Yeah, but it's way too far away to see us," Chris
said, the disappointment obvious in his voice.

"I wonder where it's going," I said absently. The
helicopter was a good distance away, and moving
fast. It appeared to be following the river, just nearing
it at this point. Had we been on the banks, it probably
would have seen us.

An instant later, it was gone, down the river south-
west of us. We both listened intently until the sound
of its rotor blades had vanished altogether.

"It's probably looking for us," Chris said bitterly.
"And now we're stuck out here for the night."

I thought about what the counselors must be thinking right about now, wondering what had happened
to the two of us. Then I thought about how we'd left
the canoe on the bank. Surely, they'd realize we were
all right, when they saw how we'd beached the
canoe.

"You know, we should have left a note or something, telling everybody we were okay," I mused.

"Yeah, and what were we supposed to write with?"
Chris asked.

"We could have written something in the sand beside the canoe."

"I guess," Chris said.

"Oh well," I said, turning away from the river again.

"They'll figure out that we're all right eventually."

"Sure," Chris said confidently. "They'll find the canoe and realize what happened."

We plowed along. It was really starting to get dark. If we didn't find a place to camp out for the night soon, we'd be forced to just bed down in our tracks. I started to hurry a little.

After what seemed like an eternity, I finally spotted a very small mound of earth, with an outcropping of rock on one side. "This'll do," I said as we approached it. The outcropping hung out just enough that, if it started to rain, we'd be protected a little. Plus, it might shelter us from the wind, provided it came from the north or the east.

Chris shivered a little. "Man, it's startin' to get cold," he muttered.

Without another word, I quickly shucked off my windbreaker and offered it to him. "Here, wear this for a while."

He refused it. "Nah, I'll be all right," he said bravely.

"Take it," I said, thrusting it into his hands. "You can give it back when I start to get cold."

Reluctantly, he accepted it and slipped it on over his head. Meanwhile, I started to look around for anything that might serve as some sort of a cover during the night.

"Why don't you start a fire?" Chris said.

"And just exactly how am I supposed to do that?" I said, giving Chris a strange look in the fading light.

"I dunno," he said. "You could rub a couple of sticks together."

"You're nuts. I'd still be rubbing them together tomorrow. You can't really start a fire that way . . ."

"Sure you can," Chris said confidently. "I've heard of people doing it."

"Oh, yeah? Like who?"

"You know. People," Chris said vaguely.

"Like what people?" I said, still scouring the land-scape for something to serve as a cover during the night. I'd let Chris worry about trying to start a fire.

"Just people," he said. "They rubbed the sticks together until they started to smoke, then they blew on it and one of the sparks caught fire in a pile of twigs."

"Sounds like you're volunteering to me," I said, grinning slightly.

"Well, okay, I will," Chris said, stalking off. He vanished behind the outcropping.

I finally settled on a branch that had dropped to the ground with all of its leaves still intact. It wasn't much of a cover, but it would have to do.

I dragged the branch back to the outcropping. Chris was evidently still scrounging around for two sticks to rub together. As I stared at our home for the night, it occurred to me that maybe there was a better way to build a shelter than this.

If I gathered up some long branches and piled them up on the open side of the rock, we'd have a lean-to. Very crude, but perhaps better than what we now had.

Quickly, because the darkness was almost on us, I raced around the forest gathering as many long branches as I could find and dragged them back to the rock. I bundled them all up against the rock. It didn't leave much space beneath, but it sure looked a whole lot better than before.

Chris was immediately critical, of course. "What good is that?" he asked.

"It's a real shelter," I said defensively.

"Looks more like a pile of sticks," he laughed.

"It's a lean-to."

"Yeah, if you lean too hard on it, the whole pile comes down," he said.

"So what'd you find?"

Chris held out two short, large sticks in one hand and a pile of dry leaves and small twigs in the other. "We're gonna rock and roll now," he said.

"Better get started. It's gettin' dark."

Chris ducked under the branches and settled on the ground, his back against the rock. He carefully arranged the twigs on the ground in a teepee and then piled the leaves on top.

"You oughta do it the other way around," I offered as I joined him inside.

"Do what?"

"Put the leaves under the twigs."

"Why's that?"

"So if the leaves, by some miracle, actually caught fire, it would spread to the twigs after that," I said, not really sure if that was right. It sounded right, though.

Chris glared at me. Without a word, he quickly rearranged the pile. Just to spite me, though, he left a few leaves on top.

I sat down beside him, pulling the branch with all the leaves on it over the opening. It really *wasn't* much of a shelter. If the wind should pick up, it would be worthless. But, for now, it was all we had.

I sat quietly and watched Chris begin to rub the two sticks together. At first, he rubbed them back and forth in broad strokes. I almost said something, that this was a complete waste of time, but Chris realized this himself and began to rub the sticks together in short, quick strokes.

I wondered if Chris would grow frustrated when

nothing happened right away and give up. He didn't, though. Even though I knew his arms were killing him, Chris just kept rubbing, watching the sticks for any hint of smoke.

The darkness descended so quickly it was there before either of us even noticed. It worked its way through the branches, up through the ground, and into every fiber of our bodies. I was chilled to the bone almost right away.

My eyes adjusted enough so that I could still see Chris working away diligently at the two sticks. Yet even if the sticks would start to smoke, I didn't think Chris could actually make it work. He couldn't really see what he was doing. It was too dark.

But Chris persisted. He always does, no matter what the odds. If I didn't say anything, he'd probably sit there rubbing the sticks till dawn. *Which might not be such a bad idea,* I thought, considering how cold I was already. At least he was doing something to keep warm.

"Give it up," I said finally.

"No," Chris said firmly. "I'm almost there."

"How do you know that?"

"Because I can smell the smoke, that's why."

I leaned close to the two sticks and smelled. I almost fell over. He was right. There *was* something. Faint, but certainly there.

"Hey, you're right, there is," I said, incredulous.

"See," Chris said grimly. "Now if I can just get it to catch . . . "

As Chris rubbed away, I decided I had to do something to stay warm. Just sitting there was worthless. I was starting to freeze. I had no idea how I'd actually sleep. Probably I wouldn't.

I moved out of our lean-to, careful not to disturb the

branches. I pushed myself up off the ground, working the kinks out of my legs. The forest was a deep, dull gray all around me.

I'd never thought of forests as especially menacing places. They always seemed rather friendly, in fact. You built treehouses in them, played hide-and-seek in them, rode your bike along trails in them.

*So maybe this is a different kind of forest,* I reasoned. It had to be, because I was just slightly afraid of this one. This forest didn't seem like the ones I'd always played in behind the house.

This one seemed like it was alive with all sorts of terrible possibilities. I was afraid to look too hard at the dull gray that seemed to melt into nothingness before my eyes. I was afraid of what I might see.

I glanced up at the sky, hoping for some relief. The stars didn't change. They'd be the same anywhere you looked at them. There was only one problem; I couldn't see any. The sky was a dull gray, too. Now why—

"BOOM!" went the thunder off in the distance. I almost fell in my tracks from sudden fright. It had seemed so loud, so close. Now, if there was thunder, then that meant . . .

I ducked inside the lean-to. "It's gonna rain," I said bleakly, more to myself than to Chris.

"Oh, no," Chris moaned. "You're not serious, right?"

"I'm serious, Chris. The clouds are starting to roll in."

And they were. I looked out the opening. I could now catch glimpses of the full moon off in one direction, and the clouds were moving rather swiftly across its face. They didn't look like friendly clouds.

There were a few more "BOOMS!" and flashes of lighting before the rain started. Actually, the rain didn't start. It sort of arrived, all at once. The first wave came in torrents. We were both soaked to the skin in about a minute.

Fortunately, the first torrent lasted only an instant and then let up. A steady drizzle replaced it.

"I almost had it," Chris said through clenched teeth.

"Good for you," I said, trying desperately to keep my teeth from chattering. I was absolutely freezing now.

"I mean it. I really did. I almost had the thing going."

"I *believe* you, Chris."

Chris kicked away his little pile of twigs and leaves viciously. They scattered quickly, melting into the grayness. "So what do we do now?" he asked glumly.

"Freeze," I said.

"I'm already doin' that," Chris answered. "I want somethin' else to do besides that."

The first wave of rain that had pelted us hadn't knocked the branches over, but our "roof" was sagging pretty badly. Not that it mattered, really. It didn't provide us much shelter anyway.

Chris and I were both sitting up, our backs against the outcropping. I closed my eyes and prayed silently for the Lord to get us through the night safely.

It was funny, but I wasn't really all that worried. At least, not yet. I still figured that they'd come find us along the river the next day. And even if they didn't, we'd just walk back. No problem.

Little puddles started to form around my feet. All around, I could hear the *drip, drip, drip* of the rain. After a little while, I couldn't really tell if it was still raining or if the drips were just the leftover falling from the leaves. I guess it didn't matter. Water is water. It still soaks you when it lands.

We sat there, in silence, for a long time. I knew Chris wasn't asleep. And there was no way I was falling asleep anytime soon. Not with puddles around my feet. Not with wet strands of hair in my eyes. And certainly not with a wet chill creeping up my spine.

"Let's roll," I announced abruptly.

"I was hoping you'd say that," Chris said. He crashed to his feet, scattering our puny, little roof in all directions. I helped him finish the job, and then shook myself like a wet dog.

"I think I can find my way back to the river," I said, looking around me. "At least, I hope I can."

"I don't care," Chris said enthusiastically. *"Anything* is better than this."

"That's for sure," I sighed. Just the act of moving around had already raised my spirits, not to mention my body temperature.

Getting started towards the river was easy. We just walked away from our "shelter." But once we'd melted into the grayness and I could no longer use the outcropping to keep my bearings, it became instantly obvious to me that I had no idea how to make it back to the river.

I didn't tell that to Chris, though. He'd probably guess soon enough. Even though I plowed through the forest like I knew precisely where I was going, it was only a matter of time before we grew hopelessly lost and Chris discovered this as well.

But at least we were moving. The chill was starting to leave me. I was actually starting to work up a little sweat. The rain had almost stopped completely. The moon was beginning to show itself more through the thinning clouds.

And so what if we didn't actually make it back to the river that night? What was the big deal anyway?

We'd just find it the next morning, at first light. All we had to do right now was keep moving until we found a better shelter, out of the drizzle. We'd find the river tomorrow.

So we walked. And walked. And walked. After what must have been an hour or so, Chris finally voiced the obvious.

"We're lost now, aren't we?" he said. There was no hint of anger in his voice, which surprised me. I figured he'd be in a major-league funk about our predicament.

"Looks that way," I admitted.

"Exactly what I figured," he said.

"You're not angry?" I asked.

"Nah," Chris said casually. "I'd rather walk all night in the dark than hang out under that rock and freeze to death in the rain. Actually, this is pretty cool."

I shouldn't have been surprised, but I was. Chris always does that to me. No one mines the silver linings like my brother. No one.

So we continued to walk. And walk and walk. I don't even remember when the rain stopped. Maybe it never did, and I just didn't notice. The night didn't seem as cold as we walked, so the rain, when it came down, didn't seem so bad.

I had no idea where we were going, now. None whatsoever. Vaguely, somewhere in the back of my mind, a plan was forming. I couldn't exactly tell what it was, just yet. But a plan was definitely forming. If we could get to Mount Argus, I reasoned, we'd be okay.

Which is why, after about two hours of trudging blindly through a dark forest, I suddenly stopped dead in my tracks and announced that I was climbing a tree.

"You're gonna do what?" Chris asked, incredulous.

"You heard me," I said as I began to look around for a tree that was suitable for climbing.

"You're crazy," he said. "You've lost it."

"No, I haven't," I said calmly.

"Sure you have. Nobody climbs trees in the middle of the night."

"They do if they want to see where they're going."

"And where's that?"

"Mount Argus," I said. "I should be able to see it from the top of a tree, now that the moon is out again."

Chris didn't say anything back, so I figured he must have approved of the notion. He started to look for a decent climbing tree as well.

"Got it," I announced to the world when I'd spotted it. "Gimme a boost up."

Chris joined his hands and lifted me up to the lowest branch on a huge, towering tree that was easily twice as large as its neighbors. I scrambled up to a low branch.

The limb was still slick from the rain, so I'd have to be careful. One misstep and I'd come plunging down. "Better stand under the tree in case I fall," I called down to Chris. "It's slick up here."

"No way," Chris called back. "You're not landing on top of me."

I looked down, to see if he was serious. I couldn't see his face, but I'm sure he was grinning from ear to ear.

I started to work my way up the tree. I went slowly to make sure I didn't slip. It wasn't easy. Twice, I lost my footing and had to catch myself before plunging to the ground.

As I got nearer the top, I began to see more of the

stars through the leaves. It had, indeed, stopped raining. In fact, it looked as if there wasn't a cloud in the sky anymore.

"How's it goin'?" Chris called up after a few minutes.

"Okay," I called back, slightly winded. "I'm near the top."

"See anything?"

"Not yet."

Actually, I wasn't altogether sure I *would* see anything. It began to occur to me that I wouldn't get to the top of the tree, only near the top. I wouldn't be able to look over the top of the tree, only out from it.

I'd chosen well, though. Either that or I was just lucky. The tree I was climbing turned out to be a few feet taller than those around it. As I got to the very thinnest branches that would only just support my weight, I found that I could look out over the forest.

It caught me short. The beauty of the forest at night, with the moon and stars shining down on it, was a sight to behold. In every direction, there was nothing to see but an endless sea of rolling, dark green. It seemed to go on forever.

Carefully, I moved up one more branch and settled in before taking a long, hard look around me. The branches swayed slightly in the breeze. I gripped them tightly and held firm to my precarious seat.

It was impossible, really, to tell where we were. The forest flowed off in all directions. There was no distinguishing feature, at least not where I was looking. I craned my neck to look over my shoulder, behind me.

There. I was sure I could see Mount Argus. I shifted my weight slowly and turned around in my perch so I could look in that direction. Once I was settled, I gazed intently at what I'd spotted.

There was no question about it. That was Mount Argus. The peak stood out against the night sky, a dark mass that seemed to jut up from the earth and swallow up part of the stars.

But how could we possibly keep our bearings as we worked our way towards it? It wouldn't be easy. We could walk for a little while and then climb a tree again.

Then I had a brainstorm. Not a huge one, but it would do in the dead of night. The moon was fairly low in the sky, off to the left of the mountain. If we just aimed for the moon, keeping it always just slightly to our left as well, we were sure to run smack into the mountain.

If not, well, then, Chris could climb the next tree.

I looked out across the dark, green forest, my eyes traveling the distance to the mountain. It didn't seem so far away, at least not from here. But the distance was deceptive. I couldn't really tell how far it was. It could be a mile, or it could be a lot more. I just didn't know.

I sat still for a moment, staring. My mind started to drift. If we could just work our way to the foothills in the next hour or so, perhaps we could . . .

"AAAiiiiiyyyyy!"

The piercing cry split the night stillness like the call of a dying child in horrible agony. I nearly lost my seat, so badly did it strike terror into my heart. Only a last-second clutch at a nearby branch kept me from plunging into the depths below.

The sound of that ungodly cry echoed in my mind for the longest moment. I held my breath, waiting for a second cry. But it never came. Only the memory of that hideous sound lingered. It was something I would not soon forget.

"Cally!" Chris called out, frantically, an instant later. "You all right?"

"Yeah, I'm fine," I yelled back. My voice quavered, as had Chris'.

"What was that?" he called up. I could hear the terror in his voice as well. It matched mine exactly.

"I don't know, but I'm comin' back down." With as much haste as I could muster, I worked my way back down to the ground. My heart was beating furiously, and my hands were shaking slightly as I reached for handholds on the way down.

I dropped to the ground, still dazed from the eerie cry that had just split the night air. The shock of hitting the ground left my legs tingling a little.

"Cally?" Chris said softly besides me. "That thing, was it . . . ?"

"Who knows?" I answered. We both knew what it was, though. There was only one animal that could make a sound like that, in the dead of night in the mountains.

Once upon a time, people called it a panther. Today, some call it a puma, or a cougar. I guess I'd call it a mountain lion.

Neither of us were ready to face anything like that. I'm not sure what I'd do, if I was confronted by an actual mountain lion. What could you do, really? It was bigger, faster, meaner, and it had more teeth than I did.

"John said mountain lions don't hunt people. And I heard, somewhere, that they actually avoid people," Chris said finally.

"Yeah, and where'd you hear that?" I asked.

"Around," answered Chris. That was his usual answer whenever I challenged him on vague pronouncements.

"Well, I'll bet you didn't hear that around *here*," I muttered.

"So what are we gonna do now?" Chris asked nervously.

"Keep moving," I said confidently. "I spotted Mount Argus, not too far away from here."

"And what are we supposed to do when we get to the mountain?"

"Find a place to sleep, I guess. I don't know about you, but I'm dead tired."

Chris just nodded. We were both out on our feet, and real thirsty, but neither of us felt like dropping right here in our tracks. Especially not right now, not with that cry still lingering in the cool, night air.

It was harder to spot the moon from the ground, but I discovered that I could make it out between the leaves once I started walking. It would disappear for a moment, and then reappear through a break in the tree branches.

We set off, glancing back and forth between the ground and the moon. I was actually beginning to feel like we were making progress. But we'd have to get closer to the mountain before the moon moved across the sky too much.

I glanced over at Chris. Despite the hour, and our predicament, he actually seemed to be enjoying himself. He bounced along beside me, hopping over logs and ducking under branches with enthusiasm. *He's clearly gotten his second wind. Amazing, simply amazing.*

At some point over the next hour, it became just a little harder to walk. Not much, but enough. That meant only one thing. We were approaching the mountain. We were beginning to work our way up into the foothills.

"Now what?" Chris said after we'd been trudging uphill for a little ways.

"I got us this far," I said. "Now it's your turn to think of something."

"Oh, that's just great," Chris said. "Give me the hard part."

"Just keep your eyes peeled for a place we can camp out for the rest of the night," I growled.

It became harder to walk. We were clearly going uphill now. In fact, I was beginning to lose sight of the moon now. It had drifted too low to see. But as long as we continued walking uphill, I figured we were okay.

"Yes!" Chris exclaimed a few minutes later.

"What?" I asked, trying to follow his gaze.

Chris pointed at something just off to his left. I stared intently at what he was looking towards, but it still took me a moment to spot it—a dark, black opening in the side of the hill.

"All *right*," Chris said. "Now we can hit the sack."

"Hold on a sec," I said, grabbing Chris's arm. "You sure about this?"

"Yeah, what's the problem?" he asked, trying to free his arm. "Let's go check it out."

I held my ground. I wasn't going near that cave. No way. Caves aren't always empty, not in the mountains. Animals use caves to sleep in, too. Animals like foxes. Or mountain lions.

"What if . . . ?" I asked, leaving the question hanging in the air.

Chris looked at me like I was crazy. He knew what I was thinking. "You've gotta be kidding, right? Out of all the caves in the whole place, this is gonna be the one the mountain lion sleeps in? Are you out of your mind?"

I still didn't budge. "And why *can't* it be the mountain lion's cave? It's gotta sleep somewhere."

Chris just scowled. "Well, first of all, we don't even know for sure that there is such a—"

"Come on," I interrupted. "You heard that thing, just like I did."

"Okay, well, anyway," he continued, a little less certain now. "There must be a zillion caves around here. What are the chances that this particular one happens to be the place where that dumb mountain lion sleeps?"

I shrugged. "Beats me. But I don't think there are a zillion caves around here. How many have you seen so far? I've only seen one. This one."

Chris glanced back at his find, wavering just a bit. "I *know* there are a zillion caves in the mountains. I just know it." I'm not sure who he was trying to convince—me, himself, or the mountain lion.

"Well, if you're so sure, then you go in first."

For just a brief instant, fear lingered around Chris. Then it vanished just as quickly. "All right, I will," he announced, wheeling and moving off smartly towards the cave. I trailed behind.

Once he'd arrived at the mouth of the cave, though, Chris didn't just bolt inside. He stopped at the edge and tried to peer in through the darkness, which wasn't of much use.

My muscles were tense. I was ready to turn on my heels and sprint away at the first sign of any movement from within the cave. Not that it would have done much good, if there really was a mountain lion in there. I was quite sure it could catch us rather easily.

"Hallooooo!" Chris suddenly called out. The sound of his voice didn't echo inside the cave, which meant it didn't go back very far. He was answered with a deafening silence.

Chris turned, then, and extended one hand towards the cave, like a waiter beckoning a guest towards a table in a restaurant. I moved hesitantly in that direction. "You're lucky," I mumbled.

"I knew it all the time," he said, clearly savoring the moment.

I ducked my head as I entered the cave. It was stuffy inside. I couldn't really tell how far back it went, and I wasn't about to go exploring to see. As long as we were out of the night air, that was fine with me.

There was sort of a funny smell inside, but I couldn't tell exactly what it was. Kind of salty and sweet at the same time, with a touch of locker room staleness thrown in. I couldn't place it at all.

"What's that smell?" I asked Chris as he entered.

"I don't smell anything," Chris said, wrinkling his nose.

"You don't?"

"Nah," he said, looking for a place to lie down. "Smells like the inside of a cave to me."

I wasn't satisfied. Despite my pledge not to explore, I moved towards the back of the cave. The smell got stronger. It was very distinct, now. It reminded me of what our bedroom smelled like at home after Chris and I had played a fierce game of indoor basketball.

"You sure you don't smell anything?" I asked Chris again, as I tried to make out what, if anything, was in the cave.

"Would you just go to sleep, for cryin' out loud," he answered. "If there was anything in here, we'd have run across it by now."

"Maybe," I said, more to myself than to my brother. It was frustrating, because it was pitch black away from the mouth of the cave. I couldn't make out anything, not even where the cave actually ended.

I stepped on a couple of sticks, which I kicked away. They landed with a soft *thunk* a few feet away. I was sure the smell reminded me of something, but I just couldn't place it. It would come to me, though.

"Come on, Cally, you're keepin' me up," Chris said.

Reluctantly, I turned away from the back of the cave and came back towards the front. Chris had already stretched out against the side of the wall.

"Chris, I guess you were right," I acknowledged as I found a place to sleep on the other side of the mouth of the cave.

"Just lucky," he said. "By the way, here's your windbreaker. I'm warm now. Thanks." He tossed the windbreaker over to me. It smacked me in the face before I could catch it.

"You're welcome," I said, donning it quickly. I was a little chilled, and the windbreaker felt good.

I tried to settle in, resting my head on one arm. It was very uncomfortable. But this was infinitely better than wandering around in the moonlit dark, with water constantly dripping down on us from the leaves.

After what seemed like hours, I could finally feel myself drifting off. Or, at least, I wasn't so wide awake that I could hear every single sound the night made.

For some strange reason, I started thinking about the dog our family had had down in Alabama—a golden retriever my father had—that had died of old age before Susan was born.

The dog had been absolutely terrified of lightning. Whenever a storm raged outside during the middle of the night, that dog would come into my room and curl up beside me on the bed. It wasn't allowed to do that, but I didn't mind and I never told anyone.

I don't know why I was thinking about that old dog.

But every time a storm came over, and the thunder boomed outside our house, it would come slinking into my room, its whole body tense with fear. Sometimes, it was shaking so badly I wondered how it could walk.

I closed my eyes, trying to picture that retriever. It had the sweetest eyes. It always loved to play catch with a ball. It would fetch it endlessly, charging all around the yard.

Just before I drifted off, I could see the dog lying beside me on the bed, that funny smell of fear lingering in the air as it curled up beside me on the bed . . .

"NO!" I yelled at the top of my lungs, bolting straight up. For a moment, I couldn't get my bearings. A dull light was just starting to enter the cave. I had no idea how long I'd been asleep, but some terrifying thought had driven me from my slumber.

"What's wrong?" Chris asked, rubbing his eyes. I'd woken him, and I don't think he was real happy about it.

"I . . . I don't know," I said, rubbing my eyes too. "Something. Something scared the bejiggers out of me."

"So what was it, already?"

"I was having this dream. No, it was a nightmare . . . "

" 'Bout what, already?"

"Our old dog. The golden retriever."

"Yeah, and so what?" Chris asked, clearly exasperated.

"The dog was climbing up in bed with me. You remember, the way he always did when there was thunder and lightning outside?"

"Wow. What a nightmare," Chris laughed.

"No, wait," I said impatiently, ignoring his barb. "There was something. I was dreaming about that, about how it would curl up beside me." My mind drifted off for a moment. "His fur in my face. A funny smell. Reminded me of ... "

I suddenly remembered. I jerked my head around towards the back of the cave, making the connection now. The smell. It was the same smell. I was sure.

"What?" Chris asked, staring at me as if I'd lost my mind.

"It was exactly the same," I said absently, trying to see the back of the cave through the early morning light.

"*What* was the same, you peabrain?"

I didn't answer, because my eyes had spotted something. One of the sticks I'd stumbled over in the dark earlier that night. It was lying just a few feet away. But it didn't really look like a stick. It looked more like a ...

"Chris!" I whispered fiercely. My blood had stopped running through my veins. My heart had stopped beating in mid-pump. I felt like I was suffocating on the air I was now breathing.

"What? Why are you whispering?"

"Look!" I hissed. I pointed towards my discovery. Chris swiveled around and looked at it too. He recognized it instantly, as I had. A bone. A very large bone, with one end gnawed off.

Chris instinctively jerked away from it, scrambling across the cave on all fours. He crashed into me and held tight. I didn't budge. Somebody still had their hand on the freeze-frame button that controlled my vital organs.

We both stayed there for a very long moment, our eyes glued to that bone, our minds paralyzed by the thoughts it conjured up. We both knew what that gnawed-off bone meant.

Chris stirred finally. "We gotta get outta here!" he said fiercely. He started to bolt towards the opening of the cave. I reached out at the last instant and grabbed his arm.

"Wait. Not just yet," I hissed.

"Let's go!" he said, his voice starting to rise with panic.

"No," I said firmly, refusing to release my grip.

"Lemme go!" Chris tried as hard as he could to free himself. I grabbed one of his legs with my free hand and pulled him to the ground, like a cowboy roping a stubborn steer.

"Listen!" I said through clenched teeth. "Mountain lions hunt at night. They return at daybreak."

"So?" Chris said dully.

"So, if this is the lion's cave, he'd know we were in here. He wouldn't just come charging in. He'd wait outside. He'd wait for us to emerge, and then pounce on us."

Chris shivered. He was probably thinking about that, about this mountain lion jumping on his back as he ran away from the cave. "So what do we do now?" he asked. "Just stay in there forever?"

"I don't know." I relaxed my grip. Chris wasn't going anywhere. Not now. "We've gotta figure out a way to see if he's out there."

"How're we gonna do that?"

I tried to picture the mountain lion, see him through the dull light. He'd be out here, lying down in the bushes, staring intently for any sign of movement at the mouth of his cave. Would he react to that? Would he jump at it?

An idea hit me like a runaway freight train. Before I could even think it through, I pulled the windbreaker over my head. I took a deep breath and then scram bled over to the bone the lion had been gnawing on. My hands trembled just a little as I picked it up.

"What are you doing?" Chris asked.

"We need a decoy," I said, gripping one end of the long bone. I placed the hood of my windbreaker on the other end and held it out in front of me. That should do the trick, I thought.

"A decoy? What for? That dopey old thing won't scare the lion away."

"No, but if you'll keep quiet for a second, I can listen for any sound when I put it outside the cave."

Chris didn't say anything. He watched me in terrified fascination. He eased himself into a crouching position, just in case he had to run. Not that there was really anywhere to run to, I thought grimly. The lion had us right where it wanted us. We'd wandered into its den like fools.

Try as I might, I couldn't keep my arm from shaking as I pushed the windbreaker out into the open. I listened for all I was worth, trying to pick up any kind of sound, any kind of movement outside the cave.

As I eased the windbreaker out into the open, I peeked out the side of the cave. I couldn't see much. But I didn't care about that. I was listening for some sign of the lion's presence nearby.

There was an almost inaudible *swish* an instant later. Like the grass blowing in the gentle breeze. Like a few leaves bending before the wind in the treetops. Like a waiting lion rising to its haunches, preparing to leap.

I froze. The windbreaker hung out in front of me, limp. I stared for all I was worth.

There was the tiniest of movements about fifteen feet away, directly in front of the cave, right in my line of sight. It was just a very tiny movement, not much of anything at all. But enough to make me wonder.

I stared at that spot for as long as I dared. I imagined that I could see a patch of brown through the dark, green leaves. But I couldn't be sure. Not really. There was no way to know for sure.

I pulled the windbreaker back inside quickly, before the thing could react. I listened intently, but I heard nothing more.

"Well?" Chris asked.

"I'm not sure," I said, thinking frantically. "I thought I heard something. Then I thought I saw something, not too far away, in front of the cave."

I could see the fear in Chris' eyes. "Cally, you gotta do something," he said insistently.

My mind whirred. Another idea lodged itself somewhere in the recesses of my brain. "Okay," I said firmly, trying to convince myself as much as my brother. "If we show fear right now, that's it. It's over. It'll charge, if it's really out there."

"For cryin' out loud, Cally, how are we gonna convince that lion we're not scared out of our minds?"

"It's like tennis," I said, falling back on something I understood. "Remember? Even when you're scared stiff, you still have to act like you're not, or else your opponent will murder you? Well, that's what we have to do here."

"But how do we do that. This isn't a tennis court."

"I know that," I said intently. "But we can do something the lion won't expect, something that no animal in the forest would do. It might just throw the thing for a loop, and let us slip away."

Chris waited. I pulled the windbreaker back over my head, and then gripped the bone just a little bit harder. The throw would have to be perfect. Absolutely perfect.

"Okay," I said, trying to keep the fear from my voice. I wasn't real successful. "Here's what we do. I'm going to throw this bone right at the spot where I saw something. If the lion's there, I'm gonna nail it right in the head—"

"Come on, Cally, you're crazy."

"No, listen, this'll work. Trust me. I really think it will." Chris didn't answer, so I continued. "No other animal would throw something at it, so that should hold it for a second. But we aren't going to wait. We'll both charge out of here right after I let the bone fly. Got it?"

Chris nodded numbly, not quite sure if he believed me. I wasn't quite sure I believed me, either.

I was gripping the bone so hard now it was beginning to slip out of my hand. I eased off slightly, closed my eyes, and said a silent prayer. Then I moved towards the front of the cave again.

"Okay, Chris, when I let it loose, I want you to follow me out of the cave. Yell at the top of your lungs and run straight to the left. Run as fast as you can."

"What do we do if it chases after us?"

I paused for a second, my hand poised for the throw. "I don't know, Chris. Let's just hope it doesn't."

"Cally, wait." There was some urgency in his voice. I turned and faced my brother again. "I wanted to know. Did you just say a prayer?"

"Yes, I did," I said, meeting Chris' steady gaze. "Now, are you ready to go?"

"Yeah, let's do it," he said, some of the fear gone.

I took a deep breath, turned towards the opening, and stepped outside. Without hesitating, I let the bone fly towards the spot I'd seen the brown patch, and then charged out, yelling at the top of my lungs.

Chris followed an instant later, also yelling.

The bone flew straight and true, hitting its mark. I heard a soft *plunk*. Our voices thundered out in unison in the still, morning air. Birds bolted from the treetops. Water flew from the leaves as we crashed through them.

Something leapt away from us, away from the spot where the bone had vanished into the bushes. I couldn't see what it was. It looked brown, and huge, and fast. It sprinted off in another direction. It was gone in the blink of an eye.

Our own efforts to run away paled in comparison to the grace and speed of that animal, whatever it was. It had reacted instinctively, just as I'd hoped. It had bolted away from our crazy, lunatic charge.

But it would be back. I was sure of that. Whatever it was, it was curious now. Someone had spent the night in its home, and the animal would track us just to see what had gotten away. It would be a very, very long way home now.

# 11

**I'd never really thought much about** the simple act of the sun rising each morning. It just happened, and I didn't pay any attention to it. I sure did today, though. It was like a friend coming up over the hill to meet me, a friend I hadn't seen in ages.

Chris and I hadn't stopped running for almost a mile, even though I was sure the animal—whatever it was—hadn't followed us. At least, not so that we could tell.

We crashed through the bushes, careened around trees, and generally woke the entire forest up with our mad dash away from that cave in the light of dawn.

We were now thoroughly lost in the forest, of course. I didn't have a clue where we were. I knew we were somewhere in the vicinity of Mount Argus, but I wasn't quite sure how we were supposed to know exactly where to cross the mountain.

It was funny, but trying to cross a mountain wasn't anything at all like what I'd imagined. I thought it would be a simple matter. You come to the foot of the mountain, climb for a while, and then you cross over. No way. It doesn't work like that.

We'd gotten to the foot of the mountain, all right. We were climbing, all right. But the foot of the mountain was miles wide. And there was no way to tell through the trees where the top was.

For all I knew, we were climbing up and over just a smaller peak in the mountain range. How could you tell if you'd actually crossed over Mount Argus and not some lesser peak miles away? Beats me.

I had a funny feeling that once we were on top, we still wouldn't be able to tell where we were. Not really. We'd be in the middle of a thick stand of trees atop some peak, but I doubted now that I'd be able to see the camp to the north.

So I figured we'd just keep climbing, until we couldn't climb anymore, and hope we were in the right place. What other choice did we have? None.

Chris didn't say much, even after we'd stopped running and started climbing again at a more leisurely pace. He was deep in thought and concentrating intently on the task at hand. I left him to his thoughts.

By mid-morning, I was absolutely starving. It had been almost a full day now since either of us had eaten anything. My stomach was growling and grumbling. I told it to be quiet. It didn't pay any attention.

I thought briefly about foraging for berries or nuts, but quickly threw out that idea. I didn't know a good berry from a bad one. And the thought of munching away on an acorn didn't appeal to me somehow.

Even if we found water to drink, there didn't seem much chance of catching a fish with our bare hands. I seriously doubted whether either of us would eat it raw, anyway. At least not today.

So what did that leave? We weren't likely to run across a Burger King anytime soon. As far as I knew, it wouldn't do much good to eat the bark off trees or munch away on the grass. Which meant that we'd just have to tighten our belts a little and hope we made it back soon.

As the day started to get warmer, I took off the

windbreaker and tied it around my waist. Man, was I thirsty. Chris and I continued plugging away, step by step, still working our way upwards.

We were walking through pristine, virgin forest now. There was no sign, anywhere, that humans had passed this way before. At least not that I could tell. There were no rusted-out Budweiser cans lying under trees, or old cigarette wrappers on the ground.

At some point, I thought fleetingly about climbing a tree again to see if I could tell where we were. But the trees were tall and straight here. It would take quite a climb to get to the top of one and try to look out over the mountain range.

"Let's take a break," I said finally.

"Great," Chris said, and dropped to his back almost instantly.

I joined him on the ground, staring up at the trees, catching glimpses of the deep blue sky through the leaves.

"You know," I said, "this isn't so bad now."

"Nah," Chris said. "I sort of like it."

"But, man, am I hungry. And thirsty."

"Me, too."

"So what do we do about it?"

Chris sighed. "Starve, I guess."

"At least until we get back home."

Chris rolled over and looked over at me. "You think we're gonna get home okay?"

"Sure," I said confidently. "No problem. We just keep working our way up and over this mountain, and we'll get there."

Chris looked at me for a long moment. "Cally, where *exactly* is this mountain you keep talking about? All I see around here are a bunch of trees. I don't see a mountain anywhere."

"We're walking uphill right now, aren't we?"

"So what?" Chris said, shrugging. "When we aren't walking uphill anymore, does that mean we've made it to the top?"

"Yep, it does."

"And does that mean we've made it to the top of Mount Argus?"

"I guess so," I said, less confident now.

"But you're not really sure, are you?"

I sort of grimaced. "Well, no, I guess I'm not really sure of that. But I think it's right."

Chris started laughing. It took me by surprise. "That's about what I figured. We're lost."

"No, we're not," I said defensively. "We're climbing the mountain."

"We're climbing a mountain, all right. We just don't know which one."

I didn't try to answer. Chris was right, of course. I really had no idea where we were.

"I figure the mountain lion's going to track us," I said after a little while.

"I do too," agreed Chris. "That's what I've been thinkin' about all morning."

"Yeah?"

"I've been tryin' to think about what we're gonna do tonight, when it's pitch-black dark and that thing comes up on us."

"You got any ideas?"

Chris nodded. I could see the fire in his eyes. He'd been thinking about it, all right. And he had a plan.

"We need weapons," he said.

"Right, and how do we manage that?"

"No problem," Chris said eagerly. "The first thing we do is find some good, strong branches."

"Then what?"

"Then we break 'em off the tree, strip all the little twigs off of them and start to make a sharp point at one end."

"I get it," I said, nodding. "We get a flat rock and sharpen the end—"

"We can do it while we're walking," Chris interjected. "Then if that dumb, old lion comes around, we just give it the old one-two."

I laughed. "The old one-two?"

"Yeah, you first, then me."

"And that'll do the trick, scare him away?"

"Maybe. Why not?" Chris said defensively.

"You have anything else in your plan?"

"Yep," he said quickly. "I'm *sure* I can build a fire now. I've been thinkin' about that all morning too."

I tried not to let Chris see my smile. He'd tried so valiantly the night before, only to have his hopes dashed by the rain. Well, maybe he could start a fire. Who knows? And maybe it wasn't my mom who took that tooth out from under my pillow when I was six, maybe it really was the tooth fairy.

"And how will you do it?"

"I'm gonna gather up a whole bunch of dry leaves while we walk today, stuff 'em in my pocket, and then crinkle 'em into a million pieces tonight. That way, when I get something going with the sticks I'm rubbin' together, I can make the fire catch right away on the dried leaves."

I nodded, surprised. That almost sounded like it might work. "Anything else?"

"Well, if we make it through the night—"

"We will," I said firmly.

"We have to find a stream, or a creek, or something, when we start down the side of whatever mountain it is we're climbing right now. We can't just keep wandering around in the forest forever."

"I guess you're right," I admitted. "And a stream would eventually take us back to something."

"I know I'm right," Chris said confidently.

"You do, huh?"

Chris was staring up at the sky. "You know, Cally, I'm gonna make up for it."

"Make up for what?" I asked, not quite sure what Chris was talking about.

"Wreckin' the boat, I mean. I didn't know we'd get into so much trouble if we went the other way." Chris was clearly pretty miserable, which was hard for him.

"Chris, there's no way you could have known," I said. "No way."

"Ah, I know that. But I feel so crummy about it, like I really messed up and now we're lost and we have this mountain lion breathin' down our backs and we haven't eaten anything in a couple of days ... "

The clod of dirt that I'd scooped up while he was feeling sorry for himself made a nice arc through the air and landed squarely on his nose. It was a perfect shot. A few pieces of dirt trickled into his mouth.

"Hey! What was that for?" Chris asked, sputtering.

"Quit bein' so dopey," I said. "The world isn't going to end. We'll get home all right."

"I *know* that," he said defensively. "I was just ... "

"Bein' dopey," I said. "And, anyway, you don't have to explain to me. When you make a mistake, you can ask God to forgive you."

"Yeah, well, it's just slightly easier to talk to you," Chris said with a cockeyed smile, traces of dirt still smudging his face.

I hopped to my feet, suddenly bursting with energy. I liked Chris' plan. It gave us something to aim for, which was a whole lot better than just wandering up and around whatever mountain we were actually on. "We'd better get started again," I said.

"Oh, all right," Chris groaned.

"We can look for spears while we walk." I started to trudge up the hill again. Chris followed, reluctantly.

Chris spotted his weapon first. He plucked it from a tree that had fallen to the ground. The staff was about his height, maybe a few inches shorter. It had been fairly easy to break off.

"Make sure it isn't too brittle," I warned.

"And how do I make sure of that?"

"Bend it a little, see if it breaks."

Chris frowned. "That's goofy. Why would I want to break it myself?"

"Would you rather have it break now, or break when you're fighting that mountain lion?" I asked, shaking my head sadly.

"Oh, I get it," he said, nodding with enthusiasm. "Make sure it's tough enough right now."

"Before you actually have to use it, that's right."

Chris bent the bough gingerly, fearful that it might snap in his hands. But it bent easily, not stiffly, and didn't break. "Great!" he said. "This'll work."

"Let me see it," I said, holding out my hand. Chris handed it over warily, not sure what I had in mind.

I took it and peeled away one end. I looked at the wood carefully. Most of it was still green inside the bark, which was good. The tree Chris had plucked it from obviously must have fallen rather recently.

"So, does it meet your approval?" Chris asked.

"It'll do. Now, I just have to find mine."

Chris found a flat rock to sharpen his stick on before I'd spotted my own weapon. He started in, rubbing one end vigorously back and forth across the rock while we walked.

At last, however, I found the kind of limb I was looking for, hanging just above my head from a young pine tree. I jumped up off the ground, grabbed hold, and pulled hard. The limb bent, but didn't break. I had to work it back and forth before I could finally pull it free from the tree.

I didn't look for a rock to carry with me right away. Chris was absorbed in his task, rubbing back and forth. He wasn't making a whole lot of progress, though. At the rate he was going, it would be nightfall before he actually had a sharp point.

We needed something else, a jagged rock face jutting out of the ground that we could rub the sticks across. When Chris and I were younger, and we'd just finished a Popsicle, we'd rub the ends of the sticks back and forth across the sidewalk until we had a sharp point. That's what I had in mind. I was pretty sure it would work.

We had to walk for about half an hour or so, but I finally came across a flat, moss-covered rock anchored in the soil. I scraped away the moss with my shoe and knelt down. It would work.

"What's up?" Chris asked, still rubbing away.

"You very far on your stick?" I asked.

Chris glanced down at me, then down at his stick. It was clearly slow going. He'd only just begun to angle off one side of the end. "Not really," he answered.

"I have an idea."

"So let's hear it already."

"Well, I was thinkin' that maybe we could work our sticks back and forth across this rock here."

Chris looked at me. Then his eyes lit up. "Just like we used to do with our Popsicle sticks!" he said excitedly. It's scary how we think so much alike at times.

"Exactly. I figured we could get the rough edges out

and then use a rock to really make it sharp while we walked."

"Man, that's a great idea." Chris knelt down beside me and began to work at his stick with renewed vigor. He'd been a little discouraged, but this gave him renewed hope.

In fact, it was only a matter of about ten very intense minutes or so before we had our sharp points. The end of my "spear" was almost gleaming by the time I'd finished.

"Perfect!" Chris said with a flourish, holding his handiwork up proudly. "This oughta make that lion think twice."

I glanced down at my own stick more dubiously. I wasn't convinced anything would make the lion think twice before it charged at us. We were sitting targets. But we couldn't just give in without a fight.

As we walked, Chris moved into the second part of his plan. He began to scour the landscape for dry leaves. I lent him my windbreaker again, which he tied around his waist. Whenever he found a leaf that met his approval, he'd stuff it into the windbreaker.

After about an hour or so, he had a huge bulge around his waist. He looked a little like Mom had before she had Timmy.

Timmy. And Susan, and John, and Karen and Jana. I suddenly wanted to see all of them so much it made my side hurt. We'd only been in the forest less than two days, but it seemed like forever. I had this funny feeling they wanted to see us, too.

We walked for hours before the land began to level off finally. It must have been mid-afternoon before we made it to the top of the mountain. It seemed very strange to me. I'd thought the top would be something I would recognize. But it wasn't.

And now that we were actually up here, on top of the mountain, I had no idea what to do next. There was no way to keep your bearings, no markers to follow. We could wander forever up here and never find our way back down the other side.

I tried, in vain, to find some moss growing on trees. I remembered some story about moss growing on the north side of trees. But the trees up here didn't have any moss, and I sort of doubted the story anyway.

About the only thing that would help us would be the sun, when it started to set. But, right now, it was still up in the sky, slightly off to one side. I tried keeping it on our left as we walked, but I wasn't sure this was helping much.

I just had no way of knowing where we were. There was no way to discover the right way to go. We were now truly lost.

What was worse, I was starting to feel light-headed from hunger. It wasn't a real problem. I wasn't going to faint or anything. It just made things a little fuzzy around the edges, that's all.

Chris was oblivious to all of this, though. He was so intent on starting a fire, he was now gathering little twigs as we walked. I smiled to myself. Chris never gave up. Never. He was a true warrior. He'd fight to his dying breath.

I'd kept one eye peeled for any sign of a stream or creek, but I hadn't seen a thing for hours. The land was dry as a bone up here. The trees grew tall and straight, but their roots must have run deep into the soil to find nourishment.

A squirrel chattered off to our right, probably scolding us for disturbing its tranquil domain. We hadn't seen many animals. Birds chirped all around us, but we rarely saw them.

I'd looked over my shoulder the whole day, trying to spot some sign of a mountain lion following behind us. But, of course, the cat would track us tonight, not now. It would wait until nightfall.

Having gathered his leaves and twigs, Chris was now obsessed with finding two perfect sticks to rub together. "Gotta be dry," he mumbled to himself as we trekked along.

"Hey!" I yelled.

"What?" Chris yelled back, annoyed that I'd jolted him out of his search for the perfect fire-starting kit. When he looked up at me, I was standing stock-still, staring down at the ground at my find.

It wasn't much, really. Just a rusted-out can of some sort. I kicked at it with my foot. Most of the paper was gone from the can—just a tiny, dried-out scrap still clung to the side. But it was a sign, an indication, that human life had once passed this way. That had to mean something.

"So big deal," Chris said after perusing my find for all of a second or two. He returned to his search.

I scowled at him. I thought it was a big deal. Not a huge whopper of a deal, but something. I picked the can up, flattened it out with my hand, and stuffed it into my back pocket. I don't know why I did it. Just because.

It was easier, now, to keep going north. The sun was starting to set below the tree line and it wasn't hard to keep it to our left as we walked.

"We'd better start looking for a place to camp," I said. "We don't want to get stuck trying to find one in the dark, like before."

"Yeah, and I want plenty of time to try to start a fire," Chris said, nodding. "I think I have it all figured out."

We both kept our eyes peeled as we walked. Neither of us had any idea what we were looking for, other than that we did *not* want to find another cave. With our luck, we'd find a bear's cave this time.

We both saw the spot at almost the same instant. It was a narrow ravine, maybe ten feet across at the bottom but only a few feet at the top. It wasn't very big, but big enough for two kids to sleep in.

I thought about gathering limbs again to place over the top of the small ravine, but I abandoned the thought right away. It hadn't done much good the night before, so I saw no reason to go through the futile effort a second time.

Inside the ravine, we were shielded from the wind, for the most part. And there was just no way I could put together a roof that would shield us from the rain. We'd just have to hope it didn't rain again tonight and snuff out the fire. We had no other choice.

Chris set to work right away. He was so determined, so intent on his business, that I simply sat beside him and watched. I'd never seen Chris quite like this. He was like a madman.

First, he piled a bed of sticks on the ground. Then, he shredded leaves he'd gathered and spread them out on top. Next, he carefully arranged the twigs on top of that and shredded some more leaves for good measure.

Silently, almost grimly, he set to work on the two rubbing sticks he'd brought with him. He didn't make the mistake he'd made the night before. This time, he rubbed the two sticks together in short, powerful strokes. His muscles would ache tomorrow.

I watched him for almost ten minutes. Nothing much happened. Every few minutes, Chris would stop for an instant, touch the inside of both sticks—in the spot where he was rubbing—and nod silently, more to himself than to me.

Finally, I couldn't stand it anymore. "Well?" I asked.

"Well, what?" Chris answered impatiently.

"Is it working?"

"How would I know? I've never done this before."

"What do the sticks feel like?"

"They're starting to get hot," he said curtly.

"That sounds hopeful."

"Well, it isn't," Chris said.

I decided not to bother him anymore. I stood up, stretched my legs, and wandered around a little bit. It was already starting to get dark, even though the sun had dipped below the tree line just a little while ago. It was amazing to me how quickly night fell here.

The night concert was just beginning. The musicians were pulling their instruments out of their cases and sounding a few, tenative notes. Off in the distance, I heard the hoot of an owl. Crickets chirped here and there. Birds called out to each other.

I stood very still, listening to the world around me. It was really very quiet, compared to the world I usually lived in, yet it was not quiet at all. There was life everywhere. It just wasn't the kind of life I was used to. This was another world, one I was not familiar with.

If Chris and I had to stay out here much longer, could we survive? I doubted it. We didn't know what we were doing. This wasn't a tennis court, where I understood the challenges. Here, we were total, rank amateurs. There was no court referee to explain the rules.

Well, that wasn't exactly true. I'd felt for some time that God was watching over the two of us out here. I'd felt His presence here in a way I never could in the middle of civilization. There were less distractions here.

The simple rule here was survival. So far, that didn't seem to be much of a problem. It would be in a few days, though, if we didn't find anything to eat. We'd find water tomorrow, I was sure. But survival most certainly would be a problem if that mountain lion had, indeed, stalked us and would show up at our "camp" tonight.

I wandered back to the ravine. Chris was still rubbing away diligently. He didn't even acknowledge my presence.

I sat down beside him again and watched for a little while. "Chris?" I said, when my impatience had outgrown my ability to leave my brother alone with his task.

"Yeah, what?" he said irritably.

"What do we do if this doesn't work?"

"Freeze, like we did last night."

"You'd better make it work," I kidded.

"I won't be able to if you don't leave me alone," he said, casting a dark glare at me.

"All right," I said, hopping to my feet again. "But I sure could go for a milk shake and a cheeseburger and maybe some—"

"Would you get outta here!" Chris growled.

I wandered away again without a retort. I started to swing my arms aimlessly. I was absolutely, categorically no good at waiting. It always drove me right to the brink.

Whenever Chris and I would go for a movie, for instance, I'd wait until just the last minute to leave to make sure we didn't wait in line at the theater. If I was in a drug store to buy something, I'd wander around until I spotted an opening at a check-out line.

I'd rather do *anything*—scrub kitchen floors, take out the garbage three times a day, mow the lawn for fun, or clean up my sisters' bedrooms every day—than wait. I had the patience of a hummingbird.

That's what puzzled me about Chris right now. He had even less patience than I did, yet he was slogging away at his task with enough patience for the two of us.

But there was some logic to it. When I played tennis, if I absolutely had to, I could dredge up the patience to rally for a while in order to win a point. I couldn't do that for the whole match, but for a few points, I could muster at least a little patience.

I started to walk in ever-widening circles around the ravine. I stumbled across it north of the ravine, where I could feel just the faintest touch of a downward slope to the land.

A tiny, trickling stream. It was so small that when I crouched down and put my hand in the running water, it took a few seconds for my hand to fill with water. I brought my hand to my mouth, splashing water across my parched lips.

Boy, did the water taste good. It had a little bite to it, but I didn't mind. No way. It was liquid, and that's all that mattered. I didn't care what was in the water.

I crouched next to the stream for what seemed like an eternity, bringing handfuls of water to my mouth every few seconds. It made my body tingle. It was marvelous. I could have stayed there all night.

But, finally, I looked up and realized that I was rapidly losing the light. I scrambled to my feet and began to trace the stream back toward the ravine.

I almost lost it twice, once under a fallen tree and again under a pile of leaves. But, finally, I followed the trickle all the way back—right to the ravine, under a rock just to the north of the camp. Chris and I had, somehow, stumbled across a natural spring.

"Chris!" I yelled, thrilled at my discovery.

"Not now!" he hissed from inside the ravine.

"But you won't believe what I've found, where we are," I explained.

"Don't care," he answered.

Then I remembered. Chris couldn't leave his project, not now. That wouldn't do at all. I hurried inside the ravine to see how he was doing. "Sorry," I said when I was inside. "I forgot about what you were doing."

Chris was hunched over the two sticks now, rubbing furiously. " 'S'okay," he said. "But could ya move? I can't see."

I was standing over him, partially blocking the dim light that still trickled into the ravine. Chris was running out of time. If he didn't make this work in the next ten minutes or so, he'd lose the light. And we'd have to spend the night here in darkness.

"How's it comin'?" I asked nervously.

"Smoke," he said.

"Huh? What's that mean?"

"I've got smoke now," Chris said, almost gasping for air now. "I've been praying, asking God for His help. And now, well, I think it may be working. I've got smoke."

Chris praying? I filed that away for the moment and leaned close. He was right. There was a thin wisp of smoke coming from the sticks now. *And where there's smoke, there's . . .*

Chris bent forward again, blowing gently on the two sticks. He was trying to make whatever heat was being generated between the two sticks transfer onto the shreds of leaves.

Chris didn't stand a chance, I figured. He'd never

make it work. We were going to be left out here to the mercy of the mountain lion that I imagined was, even now, lying in wait just a few feet from the ravine, biding his time until night truly fell.

I shifted my weight, and something poked me from behind. Then I remembered the can that I'd flattened out and stuffed into my back pocket. There was something on that can. Something we could use right now.

"Hey, Chris?" I asked.

"What?"

"Could you use some paper? Would that help?"

"Boy, could I," he snorted. "But we're in the woods, remember? So maybe you could find us some matches, too, while you're at it."

I didn't say anything. I pulled the can from my pocket and carefully stripped the brittle paper shred from the can. It almost disintegrated in my hand, it was so dry. I held the prize out in front of Chris.

"Where'd you get that?" he asked, still rubbing madly.

"From that can I found."

Chris just stared at it, like it had dropped on us from heaven. Well, maybe it had, in a way. Finally, he shook his head, clearing away whatever thought had just passed through his head. "Here, hold it out just in front of the sticks," he directed. "Maybe we can get it to catch."

I complied, holding the paper just a fraction of an inch in front of the point where the two sticks met as Chris rubbed them. "You're gonna have to keep the sticks steady," I said.

"I *know* that," he said testily. "I've been doin' this for a while. You just make sure you hold the paper steady. I'll blow."

Once the paper was in place, Chris moved his pace

up a notch for about fifteen seconds and then leaned down real close and blew gently on the two sticks. Nothing. He tried it again, three more times. Still nothing.

On the fifth try, I thought I could almost see something. It was really starting to get dark. We didn't have much time, now. Only a matter of minutes. If this didn't work . . .

"Man!" Chris said. "Almost had it."

"You sure?"

"Yeah, I'm gonna do it this time," he said. His jaw was clenched, his eyes blazed. I'd never seen such a look of determination on Chris' face before. Once more, he huddled over the two sticks and rubbed them together. His hands were almost a blur.

After about twenty seconds of this, he glanced up at me for an instant to make sure I was holding the paper steady, and then leaned forward. He blew gently, softly, on the sticks.

I didn't really see anything happen. It was almost as if one minute it wasn't there, and then it was. One instant I was holding a brittle shred of paper in my hand. In the blink of an eye, a tiny corner of that shred had begun to glow with a bright orange light.

"Don't move!" Chris said. He dropped his sticks to the ground—where they began to cool—and started to blow on the shred of paper in my hands. The bright, orange line at the corner began to grow. Chris blew on it some more. The line started to turn from orange to yellow.

I could see that we'd only have one chance at it. The paper in my hand would be consumed in a split second. If we weren't able to make it transfer from the paper to the leaves, it would be snuffed out. And Chris would have to start over with the sticks. I sent my own silent prayer for help hurtling towards the heavens.

Chris gave the paper one more soft nudge, and a little flame burst from the corner. It startled me, and I almost dropped the paper. "Quick, Cally!" my brother commanded me. "Hold it up under the leaves, real close. Do it."

I obeyed instantly. I'd only have a few moments before the fire burned too close to my hand to hold on, at which point I'd have to drop it onto the ground.

Chris had done a marvelous job of building a base for a fire. He'd crumbled leaves on the ground, built a teepee out of some sticks, and piled up shreds of leaves at the top. I slipped my hand between a crack in the side of the teepee, trying to keep it steady. One slip and the whole thing would come tumbling down.

I held the scrap of burning paper right beneath the shredded pile of leaves. For two or three very long, painful seconds nothing happened. As the heat from the fire began to singe my forefinger and thumb, my heart began to sink.

And then it caught. The fire almost leaped from the paper to the shredded leaves. A moment later, there were about six or seven different orange lines glowing brightly, all at the same time. It was the most beautiful sight I'd ever seen.

I dropped the scrap of paper to the ground and tried not to yell from the pain that had nipped at my fingers. Biting my lip, I carefully worked my hand out of the teepee.

Chris, meanwhile, went back to work, carefully nurturing the birth of the fire. He directed a thin stream of air towards the glowing orange lines, turning first one and then another into something more substantial.

Finally, as I could feel the darkness beginning to

envelop us, a tiny flame started to grow. Then it moved from one place to another, and then to another. Then the whole pile of shredded leaves was burning.

I watched in fascination, now, to see if Chris had built his project right. I kept my eyes glued on the tiny twigs he'd built on top, intertwined with the shredded leaves.

I finally exhaled when I could see one of the small twigs glowing with fire inside the burning leaves. I breathed a second time when I saw yet another twig burning.

"I think you've done it, Chris," I said, my voice barely audible.

"Not yet," he said, just as softly. "There's a long way to go still."

He was right, but my joy still could not be contained. I knew the fire would not quit, not now. We had won. It was just a small victory, a private victory that no one would ever see. But Chris and I would know. We would always share this moment, as long as we lived.

And I found myself wondering, as the fire began to leap joyously from one twig to the next, if something hadn't begun to grow within Chris' soul as well— leaping joyously from one fiber of his body to the next, keeping pace with the flickering, yellow flames.

**Chris was fast asleep.** I was sure of that. He'd worn himself out trying to start the fire, which now crackled and popped beside us. So I was sure he wouldn't hear the sound.

The sound. The one I'd been listening for for over the past hour or so, ever since darkness had enveloped us.

The fire helped some. No, actually, it helped a *lot*.

I didn't mind the eyes, really. Sometimes, when the fire flickered just right, I caught a glimpse of them staring at us through the bushes. No, I didn't mind them. They were just curious about the strange creatures who'd invaded their home.

I wasn't worried about the raccoons, or the possums, or the foxes who would pay us a visit this night. No, I was listening for something else.

The sound. Perhaps it would be a twig snapping under the weight of a heavy paw, or the soft *swish* of a large, tawny body moving past a nearby bush. In my worst moments, I could imagine the low growl just before it leaped on us.

I glanced back at the fire nervously. I knew it was the only thing that stood between us and that mountain lion. "Thank You, God," I said quietly. "Thank You for answering Chris' prayer."

After a while, I gave up trying to sleep. I sat up and

leaned back against the side of the ravine, gripping my spear tightly. Chris' spear lay beside him.

Chris had been so tired that he'd only grabbed a few handfuls of the water that trickled from the spring near our camp. He just nodded numbly when I told him we could follow the stream down the side of the mountain the next day.

*If* we made it to the next day, I should have said. I gripped my spear just a little bit tighter. I added another stick to the fire, which scattered some of the glowing ashes from the fire into the cool, night air.

I didn't begrudge Chris his sound sleep right now. He'd earned every moment of it. I'd never seen him so determined. I think, in his own mind, he'd never allowed himself to think about just how farfetched his idea was. There had been one chance, and he'd taken it.

A twig snapped. Had it been, was it . . . ? Quickly, almost without thinking, I grabbed a small rock and tossed it towards the place where I'd heard the sound. The rock thudded to the ground, and a small animal scurried away.

I started to breathe again. This was going to wear me out, this constant vigilance. Maybe I'd be better off to put a few more sticks on the fire and go to sleep. The fire would keep the lion away. And if it continued to burn right through to the dawn, we'd be just fine.

No. It would never work. I'd prop my eyes open with one of Chris' twigs if I had to. I had to stay awake. I had to listen.

I began to stare at the fire, my ears alert for a movement nearby. I stared at the fire. My mind drifted. The fire flickered. The flames danced this way and that. I leaned my head back against the ravine. A twig popped in the fire. I closed my eyes, resting them for just an instant . . .

I came to with a start. A sudden, desperate chill swept through my body when I glanced at the fire. Somehow, I'd closed my eyes and the fire had nearly withered away. It was now just a mass of glowing embers. I'd let the fire burn down.

I glanced over at Chris. I could see from the faint light provided by the embers that he was still sleeping peacefully, his head resting on one arm.

My body was stiff. My right foot, which I'd tucked under my left leg as I sat, had gone to sleep. I had to limber up my arms a little as I reached for more sticks and twigs to toss onto the glowing embers.

Then I heard it. The sound. There was no mistaking it. I'd distinctly heard a guttural growl—very faint, but there nevertheless. Almost like a kitten purring, only a few octaves lower.

My mind started to race. Why would the lion give itself away like that? Was it so sure of itself, so confident it had its prey in its grasp, that it could send forth a warning?

But then, again, maybe it was trying to spook us. Maybe it needed us to bolt from our stronghold, where it could chase us down as we ran pellmell in another direction. After all, the lion had probably never hunted man before, and didn't know what it faced.

My eyes were riveted to the top of the ravine directly in front of me. That was where I'd heard the sound. It was also the logical place from which to launch an attack.

Without glancing down to see what I was doing, I tossed the sticks in my hand onto the top of the glowing embers. It would take a little bit for the fire to catch again. I hoped I had that much time.

I never really saw the eyes appear. Somehow, they

weren't there, and then they were. Two, close-set yellow eyes staring down balefully. Watching, waiting for any sign of movement or weakness. Every muscle in my body screamed to leap into action.

Yet I held my place, my eyes locked on those two orbs now peering down at me from above. Perhaps it was because, for just an instant, I was too frightened to think. I don't know. All I knew was that I felt paralyzed, incapable of reacting.

From somewhere far away, I heard my brother's steady breathing. The sounds of his slumber drifted through my paralysis like a cold bath of water cascading down across my face.

The paralysis began to leave. In its place came a white-hot fury, an anger towards this malevolent creature stalking my own flesh and blood. This lion would *not* take my brother without a fight. Never mind me. I would defend my brother to the death.

I clenched my teeth and gripped the spear even tighter, if that was possible. I started to breathe again. I could feel my heart pounding now.

Then, from nowhere and everywhere at once, I could feel God's presence. The Holy Spirit had come, in just the nick of time. I knew it as surely as I knew my own name. And what He told me was something I should have known all along, but had somehow forgotten.

This was one of His creatures. Yes, it could kill me, but that was part of the world, part of the natural order of things. That was the way it worked. Lions killed their prey to stay alive.

But we were not its prey, at least not right now. We were a curiosity to this creature. We had invaded its home, unwittingly, and it wanted to know more about the foolish creatures who'd trespassed on its territory.

It didn't want a fight, just answers.

"Mr. Lion," I called out softly. "My name is Cally. How do you do?" The lion didn't answer, of course. The pale, yellow eyes never flinched.

"We didn't really mean to sleep in your cave last night," I continued. "Honest. It was a mistake. It was raining, and we didn't have anywhere to sleep, and your cave was so dry. I promise we won't do it again. You can have it back."

My voice had a lazy, dreamy quality to it. I felt foolish talking to a mountain lion, but I really didn't know what else to do. The creature wanted to know who we were. Well, this was who we were. We communicated. We reasoned. We talked. That's what people do, mostly.

One of the sticks had begun to burn. We had a fire again—a small one, but a fire nevertheless. The light from the fire danced back and forth, occasionally casting a shadow across the yellow eyes staring down.

"Mr. Lion, you've probably never seen people before, have you? You really don't know what we are. Well, I'll tell you. We're like you, sort of. We have moms and dads, like you. We have babies, like you have cubs. We have families like you.

"We like to roll around in the grass when it's sunny outside. We like to sleep in the shade when it gets too hot. We like to fight with each other sometimes, just for fun."

Another stick had caught now. The fire was beginning to grow rather quickly. Soon, it would be back to full strength.

"So, you see," I said reasonably, "we're not so different, you and I. Our worlds are different. We're stumbling around in yours. We'd like to leave it, as soon as we possibly can. But you and I, we have some things in common. I really think we do."

There was no answer. Not even a swish of the tail. For all I knew, the lion was ready to spring at any moment. Yet I didn't think so. The still, small voice that often spoke to me told me, now, that the lion was merely curious. We were an oddity, and my voice confirmed it.

Chris stirred beside me. I didn't look over, fearful that I would lose sight of the lion's eyes, but I could still see him out of the corner of one eye. Chris rustled again, and then sat up.

"Cally?" he mumbled. "Who're you talkin' to?"

"Nobody, really."

"Yeah, you are. You're talkin' to somebody."

I didn't want to scare Chris. There was no need for him to panic too. Yet I had to warn him, now that he was awake. He needed to know what was happening here, in case we had to defend ourselves.

"Chris," I said as calmly as I could manage. "Don't make any sudden moves, but I'm pretty sure the lion is sitting up at the top of our ravine looking down at us. That's who I'm talking to."

"What!" he whispered fiercely. "Are you sure?"

"Pretty sure. But Chris, I don't think it really wants to hurt us. I think it's just curious. If it had wanted to hunt us down, it could have by now."

When he didn't answer me right away, I risked a glance over at Chris. He'd gathered up his spear, and he was moving into a crouch. I should have known. Chris wasn't about to wait for something to happen. He was going to make it happen.

"Chris!" I hissed. "No, don't do it! It'll make the lion mad."

Chris still didn't answer. He was moving into action, before he really had a chance to be afraid, before he had a chance to think about how crazy it was to try to attack a lion.

He was staring at the same spot just above the ravine. I was sure he'd seen the same pale, yellow eyes. Now in a half crouch, he lowered the spear to his side and took careful, steady aim. A long moment passed. I held my breath.

In a blur, Chris rose to his feet and fired the spear at the top of the ravine. It twisted just slightly after it left his hand. The sharp point of the spear struck the rock just inches below the spot where we'd both seen the yellow eyes and glanced off. The spear clattered noisily to the ground, harmless now.

The pale, yellow eyes were nowhere to be seen. The lion was now gone. Was it gone for good? Had it melted back into the night from whence it had come? Who could say?

"Great, I missed," Chris said angrily, retrieving his spear.

"Just as well," I said. "If you'd hit it, you'd probably just have made it angry."

"That dumb, old lion better not come back," my fearless little brother said bravely. I could only just barely hear the quaver in his voice as he spoke. "I won't miss the second time."

"I'm sure you won't," I said, relaxing a little. I had a feeling, a powerful feeling, that the lion had satisfied its curiosity. It had come and seen the strange trespassers, heard one of them speak. Like a house cat peering around a corner into another room to see what was there, it had watched us long enough to understand what we were and then vanished.

Chris' errant spear had simply been a convenient signal that it was time to leave, nothing more. I was pretty sure of this. But I would never tell my brother.

Better for him to think that he had chased a vicious, hungry lion away with a near-perfect strike of his sharp spear.

All of a sudden, for the strangest reason, the night seemed friendly. The woods seemed inviting, like a home. We were no longer strangers. We had survived the worst nightmare the place had to offer, and we had somehow crossed over a divide.

This place was now our place as well. We could live here, in peace with the neighbors. I couldn't say how I knew this. I just knew it. This was God's world, too, with all of the same rules and everything. It just took a little bit to understand them out here where no one was around to tell you what they were.

"I'm going to sleep, now," I told my brother.

"I'll stand guard for a while," said Chris, who was now very much awake. "I'll let you know if the lion comes back."

"I don't think it'll come back now," I said, yawning. "I think you chased it away."

"It'll stay away, too, if it knows what's good for it," Chris said, brandishing his spear fiercely.

I smiled to myself. The warrior was guarding the hearth now, protecting the family from all attackers. We were safe. The world was right again. I could sleep in peace.

As my eyes closed and I began to drift off, I listened to the neighbors around us telling their tales. The cricket a few feet away was now making its presence known. A bird called out from somewhere above. An owl hooted, way off in the distance.

And Chris the Brave was throwing more sticks onto the fire, making sure that we were ready for anything else that might foolishly decide to enter our own corner of the world this night.

# 13

**I was almost sad.** Almost, but not quite. As Chris and I began our third day in the wilderness, we both could feel the odyssey already beginning to end. The still, small voice told me it was time to go home. I think that same voice now spoke to Chris as well.

The lion had not come back. Chris, the warrior, had made sure of that. Never mind that he, too, had drifted off to sleep somewhere during the night and let the fire burn down to the embers, just as I had. He'd acted bravely and had chased the lion away forever.

As we began to follow the stream down the side of the mountain, Chris began to retell the story of how he'd grabbed the spear and fired it at the lion, just nicking it, perhaps.

"You nicked it, Chris?" I asked him.

"Yeah, sure, well, maybe I did," Chris answered evasively. "The point went right at the lion. I probably nicked it before it ran off."

"Maybe," I said, knowing that the story had already changed once forever, and would likely change a thousand times in the retelling over the years. Oh well.

It was hard to follow the stream, especially because Chris was still too excited to pay even the slightest attention to the task at hand. So I persevered. I got down on my hands and knees to track the flow of water on several occasions, while Chris jabbered on.

I didn't mind, really. I was glad we were going home. I was glad we'd made it through the night. I was glad we were now going *down* the mountain.

Finally, after an hour or so, the stream stopped being a stream and started to look more like a little river, cascading down the side of the hill. That made it a whole lot easier to follow.

It was a great day for a hike in the woods. If we weren't lost in the woods and I wasn't hungry enough to eat the bark off the trees, it would have been glorious.

By mid-morning, the river really was a river. It was very easy to follow now.

"Hey! I have an idea," Chris said.

I just groaned. "What?"

"Let's find a log and float down the river," he said. "It'd be great. We could move faster that way."

"Yeah, and if the river turns into rapids, we could . . . "

"Ah, it won't," Chris said, wrinkling up its nose. "It's just a puny river."

"We'd make better time if we walked," I said, knowing I was losing the argument.

"Yeah, but it'd be easier to ride. And more fun."

I walked for a little ways, thinking. Maybe Chris was right. The river was flowing downhill, and it *would* be easy to follow.

"All right," I sighed. "We'll look for a log. But if there's any possibility that we're about to hit rapids . . . "

"I know, I know," Chris said quickly. "We'll get off right away. Don't worry so much."

We didn't find a good log right away. The ones we found were either too big, or too far away from the river. Finally, Chris stumbled on a small log lodged near the bank. It was big enough for one person.

"Go ahead," I told him. "I'll find one and catch up."

"I'll go real slow," Chris said.

I just nodded as Chris eased his way into the water. "AAhh!" he yelled as he stepped into the water.

"What's wrong?" I called out anxiously.

"It's *freezing!*" he yelled back.

I just shook my head. Everything was an emergency to Chris. I continued to glance from side to side as I walked. Chris was grunting as he shoved the log into the water and began to move.

I spotted a log half buried in the mud at the side of the bank. It wasn't great, but it would have to do. I didn't want to let Chris get too far away.

I pulled and tugged on the log until it finally broke free. Then I eased my way into the water. I didn't yell when the water worked its way up my legs, but Chris was right. It was about as cold as I could ever imagine water feeling. My legs were numb almost right away.

The bottom of the tiny river was slick from the moss that grew there. The log glided easily down the river, rolling across the moss when it dipped down low from my weight. We were not, however, going to set any speed records.

But this was a little easier, if you didn't mind the cold. And if the river picked up any speed at all, we'd make better time.

Chris was somewhere ahead. I could hear him yelling at the plants and weeds that got in his way, or complaining loudly when his leg caught on something as he drifted by. I started to kick off the bottom to make my log go a little faster.

I almost roared past Chris when I finally caught him. Well, maybe I didn't exactly *roar* past him, but I was rolling along at a pretty decent pace.

"Hey! Wait up," Chris called out after me as I started to pull away.

"Catch me," I called out over my shoulder.

Chris didn't answer, which told me that he was pushing furiously at the bottom, his feet probably slipping on the moss like mine were. I tried to pick up my own pace, which was hard considering that if you went too fast the log caught on things.

The river started to widen just a little. I glanced over my shoulder. Chris had fallen about fifty feet behind. He was trying gamely, though. I eased off on my own pace a little.

After another twenty minutes or so, the mountain started to turn steep. I slowed, pulled the log to the bank, and waited for Chris.

"Wh-Whatcha waiting for?" he asked me breathlessly when he was by my side.

"You, slowpoke," I said, grinning.

"Come on. Let's keep going."

"You sure? It's starting to get steep."

"Not too much," he said. "We can always stop."

I rolled my log back in. I shivered a little as I eased back into the ice-cold water. The current caught the log and pulled it along. I really didn't have to do much to make it go now.

I moved out in front of Chris again, much to his dismay. In places, my feet didn't touch bottom now. The stream really had turned into a narrow river flowing down the side of the mountain.

My log slowed and started to get tangled up in a mass of sticks and brambles that had grown up over the river. I carefully worked my way through them, not paying a great deal of attention to where I was. I just wanted to get through.

I eased the log one way, then another, lifting a vine

here, moving a pile of sticks out of the way there. Chris had reached the same brambles, now, and was working his way through along with me.

As I broke free, the log almost shot out from under me like a steel ball erupting from the mouth of a cannon. I clung to the log as it bolted down the side of the mountain, which was now precipitously steep. There was no turning back. I couldn't stop even if I wanted to.

A few seconds later, I heard Chris yell as he, too, came bursting out of the brambles above me. I couldn't tell if he was shouting from joy or fear. Probably a little of both.

If anything, I began to go faster. I had to use my feet to kick against the sides of the river to keep the log from capsizing. I was really moving now. My body was jarred time and again when the log crashed below the water.

What had I warned Chris about? Not getting caught in any rapids? And what was I now doing?

The landscape started to blur a little. Trees were shooting past me.

Then, in one moment of fury, the water cascaded over the edge. Without warning, I was suspended in midair. The log went one way, and I went another. I tried to cry out, but the sounds never came.

I hit the water below and went down, down, into darkness. I began to panic, thinking I would never come back up. Plants were trying to wrap themselves around my ankles, gripping me tightly, holding me fast in these murky depths.

And then, in one pure, sweet moment, I broke free of the surface. I sucked in as much air as my lungs could manage. I did it again, splashing madly to keep myself afloat.

Chris came hurtling over the edge, straight at me, an instant later. I scrambled to get out of his way. His log went one way, his body another. A cry of terror did leave his throat, echoing through the forest. Then he plunged into the icy depths, as I had.

He was gasping for air as he came back up. I swam over and grabbed one of his arms to still the panic I was sure he felt. It was different, watching someone else go through what I had just experienced.

"It's all right," I said, seeing the panic still in his eyes. It looked an awful lot like when Susan was trying to swim and had fallen in the deep end, over her head, and I had pulled her out. That kind of panic.

Susan. And Timmy, and John, and Jana, and Karen. And Mom. I almost started to cry. They must be so worried, frantic out of their minds. Like Chris and I had been for an instant when we felt like we weren't ever going to come back up in the dark water. Only worse, because the feeling couldn't go away. We had to get back, had to get home.

"Come on, Chris, let's walk for a while," I said.

Chris just nodded numbly. We couldn't have gone very fast in the water anyway, because the land was almost level now. I wondered where we were. Had we made it to the other side? Were we, in fact, finally on our way home?

\*     \*     \*     \*     \*

My clothes had finally dried out after an hour of hard walking. I was dead tired, for some reason. The water does that to you, I guess. All I wanted to do was lie down and take a nap. But I pressed on, and so did Chris.

I don't know who heard it first. The voices. Like a blast from the angel's trumpet. Like the first time you hear that still, small voice call out to your troubled heart. Or like the sound of a mother coming into a darkened room to calm her crying baby.

"It's them!" Chris yelled, starting to run. I was right behind, running pellmell around trees, over logs and stumps, towards the sound of the voices. I'd recognized one or two of them.

We both burst free of the woods at the same moment. We both saw Susan and John playing catch at the side of the lake, not more than fifty yards from where we'd come out of the woods. We both saw Karen and Jana sitting together at a picnic table, playing some kind of a card game.

And we both saw Mom, with Timmy in her arms, look up at us as we came running towards her. She almost dropped the baby, so great was her joy. She was crying as hard as I'd ever seen her cry as Chris and I reached her side at exactly the same time.

We'd only been gone, lost in the wilderness, for three days. Yet it seemed like forever. How it must have seemed like to Mom I couldn't even begin to imagine.

From somewhere, I heard Karen say that they'd found our canoe, stranded on some rocks below a series of rapids. It must have drifted free from where we'd beached it. Karen said they'd dredged the river for two days, sure that both of us had drowned in a canoe accident. *I knew we should have left a note, or something,* I thought fleetingly.

But it didn't matter, not now. "Oh, my babies!" Mom sobbed quietly after a very long time. I didn't even notice the other kids around. They were there, somewhere. But I was home. I could feel it in every part of me. I was home.

Like "The Capital Crew," Jeffrey Asher Nesbit and his wife and children live near Washington, D.C. Jeff is currently Associate Commissioner for Public Affairs for the U.S. Food and Drug Administration. Before that, he worked as press secretary for Vice-President Dan Quayle and as an investigative reporter in Washington.

Jeff's into sports like Cally, and was the captain of his high school tennis team. When he was a kid, Jeff read all the time, and when he ran out of decent books he promised himself he'd write some himself someday. You'll enjoy his Capital Crew books; he's written others too, like *All the King's Horses* and *Absolutely Perfect Summer* and *The Great Nothing Strikes Back.*

**Have you read the next book in the
Capital Crew series?**

The car pulled up in front of the house. The engine cut
off. I heard the slight creak of a door opening slowly,
and an instant later a dark form moved quickly from
the car and up the sidewalk leading to our house. . . .

I slipped down the stairs from our loft as quietly as I
could, making sure I didn't step on the stairs that
creaked. I glided down the hall to Karen and Jana's
room, and hovered outside the door for a second.

Then I heard the tiny, muffled sobs coming from the
room. I eased the door open slowly and peered
in. . . . Jana looked about as sad and forlorn as I'd ever
seen her. She looked like her best friend in the world
had just moved to the South Pole. Which wasn't all
that far from the truth.

"I really wish you wouldn't go," Jana said.

"I have to, Jana, you know that," Karen said.

Karen opened the closet, pulled out a travel bag,
and then began to open all of her dresser drawers and
pull things from them. She didn't lay the things in the
bag carefully. She just sort of threw everything in hap-
hazardly. That wasn't like Karen at all.

She zipped the bag shut, glanced around the room
one more time, and then moved over to the bed. She
gave Jana a big hug. "See ya," Karen whispered.

She turned and walked toward me. I stepped into
the room, and off to one side. Karen stopped, and gave
me a hug too. I hate those. . . .

"Come back soon," I said to her.

"We'll see," she said.

And then she was gone.

—from *The Reluctant Runaway,* Book 3 in the Capital
Crew series